Asenath, Daughter of Egypt

Marilyn Kay Stout

Decatur, Michigan

© 1997 by Marilyn Kay Stout

For information write:

JENNKAY Publishers
19995 Marcellus Hwy.
Decatur, Michigan 49045

Library of Congress Catalog Card Number:97-73560

ISBN: 1-891049-02-X

Printed in the United States of America

Pronunciations

Apepi	*Aw - pep - ee'*
Asenath	*As - nath'*
Hoptet	*Hop - tet'*
Ihat	*Ee - hot'*
Ipi	*Ee' - pee*
Ipitoket	*Ee' - pee - toe' - ket*
Nikansut	*Nee - kan - sute'*
Nofret	*No' - fret*
Nophtet	*Nof' - tet*
Potiphar	*Pot' - i - far*
Potiphera	*Pot' - i - fear' - a*
Wehemki	*Wa - hem' - kee*
Zaphnath	*Zaf - nath'*
Zaphnathpaaneah	*Zaf - nath' - pay - nee' - ah*

CHAPTER ONE

"Who can find a virtuous woman? for her price is far above rubies." Proverbs 31:10

The Egyptian girl fled the room where her family ate. Her bare feet slapped softly against the stone steps as she descended to the ground level of the house. There she pushed past a servant bearing water and towels and ran along the path in the waning light. She slipped quickly into the small stone chapel near the front gate and fell to her knees before the image of Isis holding the child Horus.

"Oh widow of Osiris," she prayed. "I implore you, intervene for me. I'm sixteen years old and of age to marry. Apepi has offered me as the wife of his new vizier, and Papa has consented." The girl leaned down to peer into the stone face through the dusky light. Her long, thick black hair brushed against the stone floor. "He was made vizier because he interpreted the dreams of Apepi. But he was taken from prison!" She let the tears flow freely as she prayed in the growing darkness. "Surely you can overrule the decree of even Pharaoh."

"Natha!" she heard her mother call her pet name. Suddenly the small chapel was bright about her as her mother entered, bearing a small clay lamp. Strange shadows danced across the image of Isis and her child. Asenath knew that the heavy black lines about her eyes had run down her face with her tears. "Why do you weep?" her mother asked gently.

"Why did Papa agree to such a marriage?"

The light flickered against Nofret's blue-black wig of wool. She reached to stroke her daughter's cheek, then pulled her chin up so that their eyes met. Nofret's black eyes betrayed her cheerful tone. "Apepi has honored you greatly. Zaphnathpaaneah is vizier of all Egypt, second only to Pharaoh

1

himself. You will be rich and well honored."

"Mama," the girl pleaded, blinking her eyes as the running makeup stung them. "He was in prison. He committed a crime! How can Papa make me marry a criminal?" Asenath broke into sobs, and Nofret knelt, folding her daughter into her arms.

"It matters not what he did or where he was. He interpreted Pharaoh Apepi's dreams, and he is now vizier of Egypt. And you will be this great man's wife."

Asenath lay awake upon her bed long after the household had quieted in slumber. She considered stealing away into the night, but the fear of the unknown gripped her more than that of marrying the criminal. She slipped quietly down to the path which led to the kitchen. There she removed the clay stopper from a large jug of beer. She dipped a cupful of the pungent liquid and took a long draught. Covering the jug again she climbed to the roof garden. Her pet cat, Roke, jumped down from somewhere, uttering the soft grunt she always made on impact. She meowed and almost tripped Asenath. Roke was not a rubbing cat, but she did like to walk between Asenath's feet. Asenath stretched herself upon a woven rug beneath the stars. With Roke curled close to her face and purring softly Asenath finally found sleep.

The first rays of sunlight touched the sleeping girl's face. She awoke and slipped quietly to the kitchen again. After a drink of the cool beer, she refilled a cup. Bearing a joint of meat, several small cakes, and the cup of beer, she stepped lightly along the path to the chapel.

Asenath spread her daily morning offering before the stone image and knelt low. "Oh Isis, Queen of Heaven," she once again implored. "Deliver me from this horrible fate. Free me from this marriage." She slowly poured the beer out before the image.

The girl stayed longer at her devotions than usual, and when she emerged from the chapel the sun was fully up, and the household was stirring. Asenath mounted the steps to the living quarters of her family and found an offering from Roke on the mat before the door. She gingerly kicked the dead mouse through the slats of the balcony railing.

She found her servants in her room, waiting. Asenath's body was cleansed and her hair carefully crimped. Asenath was proud of her long, thick hair. Her mother's hair, although as black as hers, was thin and fine, so she wore a wig of wool. Her father, Potiphera, priest of the sun temple, had his head and face shaved each morning. Nikansut, aged eighteen, was shaved like his father, for he would soon be an initiate to the priesthood. Asenath's four-year-old twin brothers, Ipi and Wehemki, were also shaved but had one long hairlock which curled on the right side of the head. Her sister Ihat was still a child of eight and wore her black hair in a long braid from the top of her head.

Asenath's eyebrows and hairline were trimmed with a razor. A thick black line was drawn about her eyes. She considered her light gray eyes too close together for beauty, but the black kohl drawn in almond shape about her eyes made them appear larger and wider set. Her cheeks were rouged and her lips colored red. She was anointed with fragrance of myrrh. She stood as a servant woman wrapped her tightly with the linen undergarment, which reached from below her bosom to her knees. She was then wrapped with a linen sheath which brushed the floor. Two broad straps went over her shoulders, partially concealing her breasts. Wide gold arm bands inlaid with gems and lapis lazuli were pushed up onto her arms and wrists. Large earrings were placed into her pierced ears, and a headband circled her head. A broad multicolored collar with semiprecious stones and gold beads was fastened about her neck.

With her toiletries completed, Asenath met her family in the dining room. Each one had a small lattice stand beside his chair, upon which a servant placed a platter of bread and fruits: dates, figs, pomegranates, and melon slices. This, with a goblet of beer, was the breaking of their fast each morning.

A servant came to each with a bowl of water and a towel

for the washing of their hands. When they had finished their meal their hands were once again washed. Ipi and Wehemki rose from the meal and ran away to play, the morning sun slanting through the windows and gleaming on their naked bodies. They would wear the linen kilt only when they began to attend school.

Asenath ate in silence. When the children had gone and the servants had cleared the meal away, she fell upon her knees before her father. "Papa," she whispered, clutching his white linen kilt. He caressed her head with his right hand, and pulled her chin up so that her eyes would meet his.

She stared at him a moment before speaking. "Please, Papa. Don't make me marry the vizier of Apepi."

Potiphera looked gently at her. "Your mother and I could do no better for you in marriage than this. Zaphnathpaaneah is a powerful man, second only to Pharaoh. You will be wealthy. Your station will be exceeded only by the queen herself." He paused in his recitation and considered the girl before him. "Why don't you wish to be the wife of the vizier?"

"He was taken from prison. He's a criminal!"

Asenath's grandfather, Ipitoket, spoke. "He was indeed taken from prison. But the prison in Potiphar's home houses mostly political prisoners. They may have merely displeased a dignitary. Apepi's butler angered him and was imprisoned there. It was the butler who remembered Zaphnathpaaneah's skill in interpretation of dreams and recommended him to Pharaoh."[1]

Asenath quietly asked her grandfather, "Do you think, Pippa, that I have nothing to fear in marrying one who was brought from prison?"

"Nothing at all to fear."

****

---

[1] Genesis 41:9-13

Twelve reed boats made their way slowly up the river from On, the city of the sun temple, to Memphis, the great capital city of Egypt. Slaves manned the oars and long poles which moved the boats against the current of the river Nile. Potiphera and his family rode together on the lead boat. Ipitoket sat upon the bow in the place of most honor. Palm fans were slowly waved by slaves above the heads of the family of Potiphera to cool them beneath the blazing sun. Behind them followed lesser priests of the sun temple and their families, as well as other dignitaries of On.

Memphis stretched out along the west bank of the river for eight miles and was four miles deep. A half million people made their homes in the city of Pharaoh.

Asenath stepped onto the wharf with her family. Shaded by the great palm fronds, they walked along a broad stone paved street bordered by beautiful alabaster columns. They went first to the magnificent Temple of Apis, the Sacred Bull. There the entire entourage knelt before the colossal image of Apis while servants carried a steady stream of offerings to lay before it. With their devotions to Apis complete, the family followed the long avenue lined on each side with sphinxes to the Temple of Ptah. Here they paid homage to Ptah, the "Mind of the Universe," who, it was taught, had created all gods and men by thinking them into existence.

The families of the priests went their separate ways to stay with friends in Memphis or to find lodging at inns. Accompanied by their many servants, Potiphera's family walked along the stone paved streets to the home of Potiphar, captain of Pharaoh's guard.

Potiphar's front gate opened to a small chapel behind which was a cool flowery garden of palm trees. In the garden was a manmade pond filled with colorful fish and lotus flowers.

Potiphar's steward led the family of the priest to the stairs which mounted to the family living quarters. Potiphar's home was situated atop the barracks of the prison guard and prison keeper. These soldiers also served as Pharaoh Apepi's personal guard. Beneath the quarters of the soldiers, carved out of solid rock, was the prison.

Servants hurried to them with refreshment and to wash their feet. Asenath sat on a low chair with lion claw feet and ivory inlays. The beer was cool and soothing, and Asenath signalled a servant for several refills of her goblet.

Potiphar and his wife Hoptet entered suddenly with exaggerated cheerfulness. They bowed low before the old priest, Potiphera's father, Ipitoket. Asenath felt the tension compress the warm air of the room. She glanced at her other, who did not seem to notice. The meal was laid before them and as yet nothing had been spoken of Asenath's wedding to the vizier of Egypt. She sighed with relief and picked at her meal, downing more goblets of cool beer. After the servants had brought the bowls of warm water for hand washing and had cleared the meal away, Asenath's father finally spoke of it.

"The gods have greatly honored us that our daughter was chosen by Apepi to be wife to his vizier." He waited for his friend to reply. Asenath watched Potiphar and Hoptet glance at one another but remain silent.

"Asenath will live in Memphis, so will be your neighbor, Hoptet," Nofret exulted. "You two will have to get together to visit." Nofret's comment brought no reply from her friend.

Finally Potiphar cleared his throat and spoke. "Your daughter and her celebrated husband will be far too busy, I am sure, for the old friends of her parents. They will be making friends of their own at Pharaoh's court."

Asenath watched Hoptet blanche and squirm. Her parents were blithely discussing her marriage to Zaphnathpaaneah, but Asenath knew there was something terribly wrong. Potiphar and Hoptet were uncomfortable about her marriage to the vizier. Why?

Long before the golden orb rose over the Nile, Asenath made her way to the chapel of Potiphar, for she wanted to pray alone, undisturbed by the others. She had scavenged the kitchen for offerings and found sufficient cakes and beer. Laying the cakes before the image of Isis and Horus, she prostrated herself and wept. When her weeping could be controlled, she looked into the stone gaze of Isis. "Queen of Heaven!" she implored. "Tomorrow is the day that I will be wed to Egypt's vizier. How can I become the wife of a man who has lived in prison, whatever his crimes? Please, wife of Osiris, I beg you to do something, anything!" Asenath paused, considering a more specific request. "Let the vizier die, today, or tonight in his sleep!" She watched for reaction from the idol before her, but there was none. Casting her eyes down, she spoke softly to her goddess. "He's old; he must be to be the vizier of Egypt! He's a criminal, dirty, filthy, corrupted by existence in Potiphar's prison. I am young." She looked back into the face of Isis. "He will use me roughly, I know he will. Please help me! Rescue me from this marriage! Let the vizier die, today!" she repeated. She bit her lip. "Or tonight in his sleep," she whispered, cautious lest she should anger the deity instead of enlisting her aid.

Just as Asenath concluded her devotions and petitions to Isis, she heard voices approaching the chapel. She bowed to her parents and their hosts, who had come for morning prayers. Ipitoket, following slowly behind the others, noted Asenath's tear stained face, and gave her a gentle smile.

When the others had returned from the chapel, Asenath was already cleansed and dressed. Her servants had carefully applied her makeup, and no traces remained of her morning tears.

Asenath noted that Potiphar and Hoptet cast strange glances her way as they all broke their fast on the rooftop garden. Ipi and Wehemki ran about the rooftop until their mother sent them to the yard below, attended by their nurses. Ihat sat on the woven mat at Asenath's feet. She leaned her arms on Asenath's lap, clasping her hands beneath her chin. Ihat's wide black eyes were fringed with long, dark lashes, and although she didn't yet wear the kohl and rouge, she was beautiful. Asenath admired her little sister's loveliness.

"Are you frightened?" Ihat asked.

"Frightened of what?"

"Of being married to such a great man as Apepi's vizier?"

"I have no fear of that," Asenath said. It was true. The station of vizier was not what she feared. And she had no desire to share her real anxiety with her little sister.

"I would be terribly afraid to marry him," Ihat said. "When I marry, I want him to be young, handsome, and not at all frightening."

Asenath smiled at her. "I will pray to Isis that you may have such a husband, when the day comes."

Asenath felt a gentle nudge against her shoulder and looked up to see her grandfather standing at her side. "Come walk with an old man," he said, taking her hand and pulling her to her feet.

Asenath and Ipitoket walked slowly down the broad stairs from the garden roof to the ground and then stood for a moment for the elderly man to catch his breath. Still holding her hand the old priest led his granddaughter toward the pond.

"Are you yet concerned about your marriage to the vizier?" he asked gently.

"Yes."

"Do you know what the vizier did? He alone could interpret two dreams that came to Pharaoh in the night. None of Egypt's wise men could tell Apepi the meaning of the dreams that troubled him so. Zaphnathpaaneah alone could decipher them. He is a great man, Asenath, second only to Pharaoh in the kingdom. You need not fear him." He stopped and looked into her grey eyes. "But beware his gods. He doesn't worship the gods of Egypt, but claims that the interpretation of Pharaoh's dreams came from his gods. As a priest of Egypt's gods, I can only caution you to be careful. Be a good wife to him, but don't let him sway your heart from Egypt's gods to his."

Asenath embraced her grandfather and leaned her head against his shoulder. "I will never turn from Egypt's gods. Do you really think that's all I have to fear from being the wife of the vizier?"

Ipitoket patted her back. "You have nothing else to fear."

The morning of her wedding Asenath was primped and beautified for two hours. A wagon had arrived from Pharaoh to carry her and her family. Zaphnathpaaneah had no family, so the marriage feast would be at the palace. As their hosts, Potiphar and Hoptet were honored to ride with Asenath's family. They were very quiet and withdrawn all morning. Asenath noticed them, but soon was wrapped solely in her dread of marrying the vizier of Egypt.

The palace of Pharaoh was an enormous brick building adorned with gold, turquoise, and lapis lazuli. It was shaded by tall palms and sycamore trees and surrounded by flowering gardens of fragrant oleander and jasmine. The door entered through the tall front facade, with colossal statues on each side. The palace garden was alive with Pharaohs' children playing with their pet dogs, cats, monkeys and geese. Ipi and Wehemki were allowed to run and play with them.

The accompanying priests and dignitaries from On congregated with Potiphera's family in the immense throne room of Apepi. Alabaster columns ringed the room, and stairs the width of the room mounted to the throne platform. Likenesses of the ancestors of Apepi, slightly larger than life sized, filled the spaces between the columns.

When all were assembled, Apepi was ushered into the room. All were instantly upon their faces on the floor before him. His bodyguards formed a close crush about him until he was safely seated. Then they flanked the throne.

When Pharaoh had signalled for all to rise, Potiphera mounted five steps and once again prostrated himself before the throne. "You have honored my house greatly, O divine Apepi, to give the hand of my daughter in marriage to your vizier. May my family be worthy of such esteem." Potiphera raised himself slightly and motioned for Asenath to join him. She stepped forward and knelt low beside him.

"Rise," Apepi told them. They stood to their feet, and Asenath surveyed the king. Apepi wore a pleated linen kilt to the ankle with an ornate golden belt, to which was attached a bull's tail. His thick black wig fell below his shoulders, and upon his head he wore the double crown of red and white, looking like the open mouth of a fish, which signified the united kingdoms of the south and the north. His face was shaved except for the long chin, around which was attached a ceremonial adornment. His neck ornament was very wide and richly jewelled. Around his shoulders he wore a leopard skin cape, and in his hand he held a crook, like a shepherd's staff. Apepi smiled at the sun priest and his daughter, and his green eyes were warm.

"I could do no better in a wife for my vizier than the daughter of my good friend," Apepi told him. He held out a jewelled hand to Asenath and she mounted the remaining steps and extended her hand to him. "Asenath," the king said kindly. "My vizier is a terribly eminent man in the kingdom, and he'll have a very important job to do for the Pharaoh and the people of Egypt." Pharaoh paused and squinted. "In my bed I had strange and terrifying dreams. The gods of Egypt wouldn't tell me the meaning of my dreams. But the God of our new vizier revealed the meaning of the dreams to him. For seven years we will have fatness and plenty. For seven more years we will have dearth and famine. Because his God revealed these dark secrets to him, I have appointed Zaphnathpaaneah as vizier over all the land of Egypt, to be in charge of food storage during the years of plenty, and in charge of food distribution when famine comes."[2]

What is his god? Asenath wondered. What deity is there

---

[2]   Genesis 41:25-41

besides the gods of Egypt? And why wouldn't our gods tell Apepi the meaning of his dreams? But she couldn't wonder further, for Apepi spoke once more to her.

"Be a strength and support to him, Asenath. Many burdens will be laid upon him, and he will need you as a friend and confidant."

Asenath blushed but kept her eyes upon the king. She had not yet met the man whom she must today marry, and Apepi was admonishing her to be his friend! When the Pharaoh had finished his instruction and had released her hand, she bowed low before him again and returned to her father's side.

Two long columns of guards entered through an inner door. They marched to the throne and formed an aisle through the middle of the room, dividing the assembly. Down this aisle came dancers and musicians, who parted and formed in lines on either side of the throne.

And then he entered. He wore a thick wig of black wool that reached to his shoulders, and a simple band of gold upon his head. Instead of a collar, he wore the chain of gold given to him by Apepi, and on his finger he wore the royal ring given by the Pharaoh. His white, pleated linen knee length kilt was surrounded by a golden girdle ornamented with geometric designs. Zaphnathpaaneah.

Every eye was upon him as he walked the aisle between the guards toward the king. Every eye but Asenath's. Her father turned to watch the vizier's approach, but she stared straight ahead at the image of the falcon-headed Horus at the back of Pharaoh's throne. The vizier of Egypt mounted the steps and stood at her right side. She felt his nearness but did not look at him. She felt her father leave her side. Apepi stood smiling. He extended his hands and took Asenath's right hand and the left of the vizier and put them together. Still smiling, he said, "I give to you, Zaphnathpaaneah, the hand of Asenath, daughter of Potiphera priest of On, as your wife." Still holding her hand, the vizier bowed slightly in deference to the king. Only then did he look at Asenath, and she at him.

What she saw first and most were his eyes, eyes the color of the Nile, tumultuous before a storm. She had often seen eyes of gray, green, and brown, as well as black as night, but only once before the clear aqua blue of eyes such as his, although she could not recall when. His face was narrow, with a straight nose and a strong chin. His lips parted and she saw straight, white teeth, but he did not smile. He was taller than she by a head, so that she must look up to see into his eyes. His countenance did not betray his reaction to her. She was struck by his attractiveness. He didn't look the least decrepit or filthy. None could have guessed that he had been years in the dungeon.

The vizier looked back at his king. "My gratitude to you, O Pharaoh, for so rich a gift." He bowed his head once more toward the king.

"Good!" Apepi said, clapping his hands. "And now for the feast!" The queen was escorted to the Pharaoh, and closely flanked by his guards, he led the newly married couple through a marble hall to the banqueting room. The great assemblage, preceded by Potiphera's family, followed behind. Zaphnathpaaneah held Asenath's hand in his as they followed Apepi. She knew that her palm was moist against his, and she felt the strength of his fingers around hers. When at last they were seated in a position of honor near the king, he let go her hand. They sat close together on the armless chairs, so near that Zaphnathpaaneah's knee leaned against her own, with only the gauzy film of her gown between.

When the servants had brought the bowls and towels for hand washing and the banquet was served, Asenath found eating difficult. She could, however, manage to drink the cool beer, and partook of several refills. The music was loud and boisterous as twelve women danced before the Pharaoh and the newlyweds. The women were naked except for a small golden band around their hips. They swirled and gyrated close to the king, and he clapped his hands in pleasure, smiling broadly. Zaphnathpaaneah, however, seemed oblivious to the dancing women. He looked at Apepi and spoke. He even looked at Asenath occasionally without speaking. But he did not look at the dancers.

When the dancing had ended, young girls played delicate music on large harps. The music was much softer and easier, and the beer was warming Asenath, until she feared that she may fall asleep.

It was then that she noticed Potiphar and Hoptet. They sat at some distance from her, but she could see them cringe in discomfort. She watched them for several moments casting fearful glances toward her husband.

Something stirred within her. A memory of a day long ago. She had been a child, sitting in the home of Potiphar and Hoptet as a meal was served. At the doorway, directing the service of the meal, had stood the steward of Potiphar's house. In her distant memory the face faded, but the eyes stood out clearly, green-blue as the sea. Asenath glanced quickly at her husband. He spoke with Apepi, but sensing her gaze his eyes diverted to hers.

A faintness washed over her body, a warmth not prompted by the beer. The eyes. They were the eyes that she had seen. She looked quickly away from those eyes and sought her mother in the room. There, not far away, she saw her.

"Your Divine Eminence," she interrupted softly. Apepi smiled at her. "Will you excuse me for a moment?" she asked, not letting herself see those eyes again.

"Of course," Pharaoh replied. "Only do not rob us of your presence long."

Asenath rose and walked as calmly as she could to her mother's side. Nofret's black eyes smiled at her, but sobered quickly as she saw the expression upon her daughter's face.

"Mama," Asenath said, trying to sound calm, "will you please walk with me?"

Nofret excused herself and followed Asenath from the crowded room. Asenath knew the palace well, for they had often been the guests of the Pharaoh. She led her mother to the palace chapel, which was dedicated to a number of gods. Once inside she turned quickly to her mother and grasped her arms.

"Mama, do you remember years ago the steward of Potiphar who was an Hebrew slave?"

Nofret frowned in confusion. "Why ever?" she asked.

"Do you remember him?"

"Yes. It was a terrible thing. He was the one who attempted to seduce Hoptet."

"Yes, Mama. And he was imprisoned in the dungeon beneath Potiphar's house."[3]

"Yes, I believe he was."

"Mama, do you remember his eyes?"

"His eyes?"

"They were aqua blue, and seemed to look right through you."

"Yes, I do remember his eyes. But, Natha, why do such memories concern you on your wedding day?"

"Mama, have you looked at my husband?"

"Of course I have."

"Have you seen his eyes?"

Nofret's eyes widened, but she did not answer.

"His name was Joseph, the Hebrew slave. It is he, Mama. The eyes are his. My husband is the man who tried to seduce your best friend!"

---

[3] Genesis 39:17-20

CHAPTER 2

"Whoso findeth a wife findeth a good thing, and obtaineth
favour of the LORD." Proverbs 18:22

Asenath was in his home. Nofret had cried with her, but
there was nothing that could be done. She was the wife
of Zaphnathpaaneah. Pharaoh had sent them off with
much fanfare in a royal chariot, and her family had returned to
the home of Potiphar. Servants carried her belongings into his
house, and now, with the evening falling about them, she was
alone with him.

Zaphnathpaaneah stood near the doorway. The lamps
had been lit around the room, and Asenath watched shadows
dance along the ceiling. She could not look toward him. He
approached her and held out a hand to her, but she took a step
backward.

He stopped, with hand still extended. Asenath backed
away another step. The man's brow furrowed. The sea blue eyes
looked kindly at her. "Come," he said softly, his words touched
slightly with a strange accent. "Let's sit here, and talk." He
motioned to two chairs and took a seat. He looked up at her
expectantly. Asenath dragged the other chair away from him and
sat upon it.

"Do you fear me?" Zaphnathpaaneah asked.

Asenath could not look at those eyes. She looked away.

"You don't need to be afraid. I know that you're very
young."

Asenath shuddered and forced her gaze to meet his. She
licked her lips. "I know who you are."

"Who am I?"

Asenath didn't like sitting so close to him. She suddenly
stood and moved farther away. Her husband sat still, watching
her in the flickering light. "Who am I?" he repeated.

"You are the Hebrew slave who served as steward of Potiphar's house."

"I was."

The lamps glowed in silence for several moments.

"Potiphar and his wife are friends of my parents," she finally said.

"Have you been told why I was imprisoned?

"I have."

"I don't wish to say anything against Potiphar," he told her. She still did not look at him. "He was defending his wife's honor. That's what he should have done." He paused. "As your husband I would do the same to defend your honor," he said softly.

Asenath looked at him then. She let herself look into his eyes and then quickly away.

"But Potiphar's wife didn't tell him the truth," Zaphnathpaaneah said. He stood to his feet and tried to approach her, but she stepped quickly away. He stood in the low light as near as she would allow him. She would not look at his eyes, but his voice pleaded with her. "I did nothing to Potiphar's wife. It was she who tried to seduce me, day after day. When I wouldn't be with her, she one day caught hold of my garment. I escaped, leaving my kilt in her hand, and ran away naked."[4] He was silent again for a moment.

"Please believe me, Asenath. I did nothing to her. I would not do such wickedness and sin against God."

Asenath looked at her husband. Was he telling her the truth? Yes, Hoptet was certainly capable of such a thing, she was certain of that. He sounded sincere. His beautiful eyes told her he was not lying to her. Beyond the words that he had spoken his voice had told her that he was being truthful. As she stood considering him he pulled the wig from his head and

---

[4]   Genesis 39:11,12

smoothed his hair, scratching his scalp. His close cropped hair glowed in the lamplight the color of the desert sand in sunlight. Had Hoptet condemned this man to years in the dungeon unjustly?

Asenath stepped closer so that she could see his face more clearly. He was not a youth, but his handsome face bore traces of a boyishness. "Now that you are vizier of Egypt will you punish Potiphar's wife for what she did to you?" she asked him.

Her husband's eyes widened and he dropped suddenly upon a knee before her. "Do you believe me, then?"

She must believe him. She must believe that he was innocent or her whole life know that he was not. She felt suddenly shy at his intense gaze, but she looked at him, knowing that her answer mattered to him.

"I believe you."

Her husband sighed deeply and rose quickly to his feet, taking both her hands before she knew it. "Praise be to God!" he exulted.

Asenath did not pull her hands away. She stood hand in hand with her husband and was not afraid to look into his eyes. For the first time, he smiled, and she smiled back at him.

****

Asenath awoke. At first she was perplexed. Then she remembered, and she turned to see him asleep beside her. She got up and wrapped herself in her linen sheath. She opened the door, unsure which way to go. It had been almost dark when they had arrived last evening, and she had seen very little of the house. A servant entered the dining room, in which she stood, and bowed before her. She nodded and asked, "Which way is the kitchen?"

As she descended the stone steps to the ground, she almost tripped as Roke slithered between her feet. She fondly picked up her pet and carried her to the kitchen. "Are you finding your way around your new home?" she asked the animal, scratching behind her ears.

In the kitchen Asenath found some fruit but could find no beer. Bearing the fruit she went out into the early morning. She followed the stone path that led toward the front gate. She came to the gate and then turned toward the pond. The trees swayed in the breeze and the flowers opened their bright faces toward the horizon, where the sun would soon rise. Asenath looked about her every way. Then she returned to the house.

He was still in the bed. She went to him and whispered, "Zaphnathpaaneah, I can't find the chapel."

Her husband opened one eye and looked at her. He smiled and sat up in bed. She was struck again by his sandy colored hair, and of course, those eyes. "Hello," he said.

"I can't find the chapel," she repeated.

His smile faded. "We have no chapel, Asenath."

She held the fruit out toward him. "Then how shall we present our offerings and bring our prayers before the gods?"

He swung his legs over the edge of the bed. "We pray to Jehovah, the Lord God, the Creator of heaven and earth. It was He who interpreted Pharaoh's dreams. It is He Whom I love and worship. We can pray to Him anywhere, anytime."

"I worship the gods of Egypt," Asenath told him. "I want a chapel to Isis. I go to her with offerings and prayers every morning."

Her husband reached out for her hand. "Asenath, we will not have a chapel to the gods of Egypt in our home."

Asenath pulled her hand away from him. She turned and began to walk away, but he was instantly behind her and clutched her arm. Asenath," he said, turning her to face him. "I wish for you to wear a dress like your mother wears."

She stared at him, confused.

"With cloth here," he motioned to her bosom, "that covers everything."

"That's how elderly women dress," she told him.

"It's how I want you to dress."

"Why do you want me to dress as an old woman?" she asked.

"You're my wife. It's not good that any other man should look on your nakedness." His blue eyes were kind as he spoke. "Please, Asenath."

Asenath felt bound by a great weight. "I am your wife, Zaphnathpaaneah. I must do as you wish."

His lips parted to show his straight white teeth, and he smiled again. "Would you please call me Joseph?"

"Your Hebrew name."

"Yes. I am Joseph. Zaphnathpaaneah is only a name given to me by Pharaoh. Will you call me Joseph?"

Asenath stood before her husband with her head whirling. He had just told her sternly that she may not have a chapel to worship her goddess and that she must dress as an old woman. Then he had asked her to favor him by calling him "Joseph". She was angry at him. How could he so glibly ask her such a thing? How could she so lightly answer?

But she did. "Yes, Joseph."

Shortly after Joseph left to his duties as vizier, a dressmaker arrived. She clucked and shook her head in sympathy that so young and shapely a wife must dress as a woman of age. When she had gone, Asenath, dressed in a new gown, went down to the workrooms of the household.

"Where is the beer made?" she asked the steward, who stood directing the servants in their tasks.

"We make no beer, Madame," he answered.

"Well you shall make some, now. Begin immediately. Until it is ready, purchase beer at the market. Serve it at the noon meal today." The steward bowed in response.

Asenath surveyed her new home, the home of which she was the mistress. Large, beautiful grounds went around half of the house. The manmade pond was large and oval shaped, with big golden fish and lotus flowers. The house itself consisted of servants' quarters on the lower floor and the family living area on the second floor, as well as the flat garden roof. Behind the house was a long one-storied building which contained the kitchen, stables, and workrooms. And soon the brewery, thought Asenath. To the north of the house was the well and an enclosure for fowl. To the south were the grain silos and the tradesmen's entrance. About it all was a brick fence taller than a man's head. There, in the far corner behind a thick bush, was a perfect spot in which to hide a small chapel for Isis. She would send a servant to Potiphar's home right away and ask her mother to send an Isis.

Up the stairs one entered into the main living room of the house. Large windows overlooked the city. The Nile gleamed in the sun as reed boats glided through it's silvery waters just to the west. Large water jugs on sturdy stands lined the entrance to the house. Fresh flowers were strung and hung about the jug necks daily. Designed mat work covered the floors and walls. Oil lamps of pottery were placed in triangular niches in the walls and on papyriform stands. The furniture was of rich woods inlaid with ivory and ebony. The junctures of the wooden frames were of embossed gold, and the ends of the arms had gold caps. The legs of every chair and table were the shape of clawed lion feet. One corner contained several plush cushions large enough for even a large man to rest upon comfortably. Woven papyrus screens stood upon the floor and could be pulled before open windows to allow light and air but retain privacy.

The dining room contained enough chairs for a grand feast, all arranged attractively about the room. At one end was a raised platform, or dais, upon which the family would sit to eat. The woven wall hangings contained scenes of birds and flowers. Low cylindrical papyrus stands dotted the room. Fresh flowers were everywhere in tall vases.

Four bedrooms each had a large bed and shelves along the wall for the neatly folded linen clothing and light sheets.

Joseph and Asenath's bedroom was the largest, and commanded a grand view of the city and river.

Asenath found the steward and asked for papyrus and ink. She composed a short note asking for an image of Isis, and ordered the message delivered to her mother at the home of Potiphar.

Asenath found herself waiting for Joseph's return home for the noon meal. She watched from the pond and then mounted the steps and watched from the window. Roke meowed and Asenath lifted her, stroking her sleek black coat. Her heart skipped when she saw him approach. But why? she wondered. She was angry with him because he would not let her have a chapel. He made her dress as an old woman. Still, she shivered as she heard his feet pad against the stone steps.

Joseph opened the door and found Asenath waiting. He smiled. She smiled. She loosed the cat, and they walked together to the dining room and sat in chairs close together.

"I'm pleased with your dress," he told her. Asenath hated the clothes, but she felt strangely warmed by his praise.

Servants brought the noon meal on round silver trays and placed them on two papyrus stands. Asenath waited. Joseph reached for her hand and raised his eyes to the ceiling. "Lord God of heaven," he said reverently. "Thank you for this food. And thank you for this good wife." Joseph smiled at her and reached for some food.

Asenath looked at the food and cringed. On the platters, attractively arranged, were baked fish, cucumbers, onions, and leeks. "Joseph," she said softly. He stopped chewing and looked at her.

"My father is a priest of the sun temple. The priests and priestly families don't eat fish, for it was fish who ate the lost phallus of Osiris. Neither do we eat vegetables of any kind."

"Forgive me," Joseph said. "I didn't know." He paused. "You no longer live in the home of a priest. You're my wife. Do you think you could eat these things here?"

"No. I don't eat them. Please, Joseph."

Joseph called his steward. "Zedek, my wife is not accustomed to fish or vegetables. Please bring us bread and fruit. And see that we are not served fish or vegetables again." Asenath smiled her gratitude to Joseph.

"I will see to it, Master. Here is the beer which the Madame ordered." The steward began to pour beer into a goblet.

"Stop!" Joseph ordered. He glanced at Asenath. "We will have no beer. Take it away."

Asenath waited until Zedek had gone. "Why will we have no beer?" she asked, an edge to her voice.

"I have seen beer take control of the body and mind of those who drink it. We will not have it in our house."

"A priest's family does not drink wine," Asenath told him.

"Then we shall drink water and nectars of fruit."

Tears welled in Asenath's eyes and spilled over. Zedek returned with bread and fruit. When he was gone she spoke, her voice trembling. "You forbid me worship of my gods. You demand that I dress as an old woman. But please, Joseph, don't take beer away from me. I love it. I can't live without it. Please, Joseph."

"That very fact shows why you should not have it," he answered. Rising from the meal of which he had partaken very little, he said, "Goodbye," and returned to his work.

Asenath paced the rooms of her house, twisting her hands. She needed beer to clear her head and help her think clearly. I should have asked Mama to send beer to me, too, she thought, too late.

Zedek approached and bowed. "A messenger at the gate, Madame."

"I will see to it myself," she said. Trying not to appear too hurried, she went to the front gate. There she was given a parcel wrapped in sackcloth.

Asenath peered toward the house. She saw no one, so

she hurried to the corner of the garden and unwrapped her Isis behind the bush. She fell instantly on her face before the image. "Oh, Isis! It is far worse than I imagined." She paused. "He said that he was innocent of Hoptet's charge against him, and I believe him." She peered up at the stone face, watching for some sign of assent, but she saw none. "You see how I am dressed. My husband requires me to dress like an old woman. And I will be able to bring no beer to pour out before you, Queen of Heaven. He will not let me have beer! And I must even pray to you in secret." Tears streamed down Asenath's face as she poured out her woes to her goddess. "I don't know what you can do. But please help me! You didn't prevent this marriage, so now I plead with you to help me. Let me have beer! I beg of you!"

Asenath wandered among the granaries, and there in the corner she found a large curved shard of pottery which had probably once been part of a granary. She smiled to herself as she carried it to her garden and with it formed a shelter over her image of Isis. It was not a chapel. But it was the best she could do.

The sun was slipping into the horizon when Joseph returned. He smiled at her and his blue-green eyes lit his face. They supped together as the daylight faded and the lamplight flickered about them. Asenath remembered what Apepi had told her just the day before. Could she be the friend of this man?

In the early morning Asenath slipped from bed and took an offering of food and fruit juice to Isis. She returned before Joseph awoke, and was satisfied that her devotions had not been discovered.

Three days passed thus. Asenath made her petitions to Isis each morning. She could find little to occupy her time and mind throughout the day. Joseph came home to eat the noon meal with her and returned in the evening.

On the fourth day Asenath returned to the bedroom to find Joseph asleep as usual. He continued to sleep until she was concerned. "Joseph," she called softly. "I believe it's time for you to awake."

She was startled when he reached for her arm and pulled her to him. Through a sleepy smile he said, "This is Sabbath. I will not go to work today."

She did not pull away. "What is Sabbath?"

"It took six days for the Lord God to create the heavens and the earth. On the seventh day He rested.[5] So on the seventh day we will do no work. Everyone in our household will rest."

"The servants?"

"Yes. Everyone."

"What will Apepi say when you do not go to work?"

Joseph laughed, releasing his grasp of her, and sat up in bed. "I explained it to Pharaoh. He doesn't understand, of course, but he will not oppose me in serving my God. It was the Lord God Who gave him the meaning of his dreams."

Asenath called her servants to wash her and put her makeup on her face. When the two young women came to her, Joseph told them that they would do no work this day, because it was the Lord's Sabbath, and he sent them away.

"How shall I be groomed and readied for the day?" Asenath asked him incredulously.

Joseph smiled and put his hands on her arms. "You may wash yourself." He paused. "You're beautiful; you don't need the makeup."

Anger rose up in Asenath's breast and she pulled her arms free. She scowled at Joseph, hoping that she didn't look the least bit beautiful. "I must have my makeup, Joseph." She pursed her lips and stared into his eyes unfaltering.

Joseph shrugged. "Can you paint yourself?" he asked.

Asenath had never done so, but she answered, "Yes."

"Then do so."

---

[5]   Genesis 2:2

Joseph had stood and watched the servants apply her makeup one morning. It had bothered her then, but now he watched as she clumsily applied her own. She knew the job to be less than perfect, but when she had finished he smiled at her again and led her to breakfast.

The servants brought fruits, breads and cold meats that they had prepared the day before. Joseph told them to sit in the dining room, and they ate with Joseph and Asenath, but seated on the main floor and not upon the dais.

Joseph led Asenath to sit beside him at the pond. They slipped their feet beneath the cool water and laughed as the fish nibbled their toes. When the heat grew intense, they sat in the shade of an ornamental bush.

"Your parents will soon return to On. Would you like to visit them at the home of Potiphar?" Joseph asked.

"Today?"

"Yes."

"It is Sabbath."

Joseph smiled. "We won't work hard to get to Potiphar's home."

Asenath hesitated. "I would like to see my parents. But I don't think Potiphar and Hoptet will be happy to see you, my husband."

Joseph was silent for a moment. He stared at the pond, tossing bits of stone into the smooth waters. When he looked at Asenath there was a sadness about his beautiful eyes.

"You asked me if I would punish Potiphar's wife for falsely accusing me." He shook his head slightly. "No. I was twenty years old when I was imprisoned and thirty years old when the Lord delivered me from prison. The dungeon is no pleasure. But the Lord my God was with me. The wife of Potiphar may have meant it for evil, but my Lord used it to enable me to interpret the Pharaoh's dreams. My God raised me to the position which I now hold. And my God gave me a beautiful wife." Asenath warmed at these words, and feared that her face reddened, but she didn't look away from him. "There is nothing for which to punish the wife of Potiphar," Joseph said. Asenath bit her lip. "They're afraid of you, Joseph." "Then I will tell them they have nothing to fear."

Joseph and Asenath were led to the living quarters of Potiphar and Hoptet by a servant who eyed Joseph strangely. Asenath's little brothers, Ipi and Wehemki were playing by the pond. When they saw Asenath they ran to hug her, their small naked bodies gleaming in the Egyptian sun.

The rest of her family sat in the large, richly decorated living room. Potiphar was in the yard behind the house drilling his guards, so Hoptet faced Joseph alone.

"Welcome!" she said unsteadily, bowing before the vizier of Egypt. "You honor us to enter our home. Come in and rest yourselves."

Asenath greeted her parents and grandfather fondly with a kiss. She kissed her sister, Ihat, and older brother Nikansut. Servants brought them refreshment, and Asenath helped herself to a goblet of beer, savoring the strong brew as it cooled her throat and warmed her blood. Bowls and towels were brought and their feet were cleansed.

Trays of breads and fruits were placed on papyrus stands, and servants waved large palm fans above their heads.

Hoptet signalled the steward and five dancers entered the large room. They swayed and gyrated about the room among the guests as musicians made bright music. Asenath knew that Joseph avoided looking at their nakedness. He is surely a strange man, she thought.

"Has Apepi given you the day off?" Ipitoket asked when the dancers had gone.

Joseph nodded his head in respect to the old man. "He has. This day is Sabbath, a day of rest. The Lord God made the heaven and earth in six days, and on the seventh He rested. I lost track of time when in prison, but I have counted the day that I was released as the first day, and I do no work on the seventh."

"Is this the religion of your people?" Ipitoket asked.

"It is the belief in the one true God, Creator of heaven and earth," Joseph said.

"My son and I are priests of the gods of Egypt," Ipitoket said.

"Yes," was Joseph's only answer.

Ihat squatted at Asenath's side while the men talked. She leaned close to Asenath's ear and whispered, "I think the vizier is gorgeous! I would be happy to marry such a man!" Asenath smiled at her sister's evaluation of her husband.

"Why ever are you dressed like that, Natha?" Nofret asked her daughter.

"My husband wants me to."

"Why ever, Zaphnathpaaneah?" Nofret asked, turning to Joseph.

Ignoring her question Joseph smiled and said, "I would like you to call me Joseph." Nofret glanced at her husband and Potiphera spoke.

"Zaphnathpaaneah is a very lengthy name. But in deference to Apepi, we wish to use the name given you by him. What if we use a shortened form, such as Zaphnath?"

Joseph nodded, smiling at his father in law. "If you wish."

Hoptet blanched as Joseph mentioned his Hebrew name, by which he had been known as the steward of her home. Asenath saw her discomfort as Joseph smiled at her and suggested that she and Potiphar may also call him Zaphnath.

She sat silently, trembling visibly. Suddenly she was on her face upon the floor before Joseph. "Please, sir, forgive me!" she cried. "Forgive me! Forgive me!"

All in the room were confounded. Hoptet began to weep violently. Potiphar entered the room to find his wife prostrated before Joseph. In sudden fear he was instantly at her side, bowing low before Joseph. Asenath sipped her beer and watched her husband. He reached down and touched the head of the prone woman.

"You are forgiven," he said kindly.

Her weeping subsided and she looked up at him from a tear streaked face. Her eyes still held fear. Potiphar, too, looked at Joseph.

"I believe you have suffered for your deed," Joseph continued gently. "My God brought me out of prison to serve Him. You have no need to fear."

Hoptet clutched Joseph's bare feet and began to weep again. "Thank you! Thank you!" she wept.

"I, too, implore your forgiveness," Potiphar said.

Joseph looked into the eyes of the man who had imprisoned him for ten years of his life. There was no guile in his gaze.

"You have no need to fear," Joseph said kindly. "You did nothing for which to be forgiven. You had no choice. A man must defend the honor of his wife."

Potiphar was confused. He looked at his wife, collapsed in tears at his side. "Yet," he said, trembling, "you forgave my wife."

Joseph nodded. "Yes," he answered. "I have forgiven her."

Potiphar and Hoptet bowed away from Joseph and left the room. Joseph rose and motioned to Asenath.

"We hope that you have a pleasant trip returning to On," he said, bowing his head toward his father in law and the elderly priest. He reached for Asenath's hand and led her from the room and toward their home.

As they walked along, Asenath leaned against Joseph's hand heavily. She felt deliciously warm and foggy. Joseph did not speak until they reached their home. The servants, restless from the day spent in idleness, eagerly tried to wait upon their master and mistress, but Joseph waved them away, asking only that some bread and cheese be brought to the bedroom.

The sun was low in the sky, painting the eastern clouds

pink, as Asenath stretched out on the bed with her eyes closed. Joseph stood by the bed, watching her in the waning light.

"Do you understand why, now?" he asked her.

Asenath opened her eyes. She raised up groggily onto her elbow. "Do you speak of Potiphar and Hoptet?"

"No," Joseph said. "I speak of you. And beer."

Asenath sat up suddenly. "Beer!"

"Beer," Joseph said. "You drank much beer at the home of Potiphar. Now it controls your mind and your body. That's why I don't want it in our home."

"I didn't drink it in our home."

"I don't wish for you to drink beer at all."

The warmth had burned into a fire in her veins. She stood to her feet, clenching her fists. "It was not my choice to become your wife," she said cruelly. She hoped for her words and tone of voice to wound him. "I was forced into this marriage. And since I became your wife you have required too much from me. You won't let me have a chapel to Isis. You make me wear clothes like an old woman, and everyone stares at me." His sea blue eyes did not leave hers. She watched his jaw tighten, but she could not read his thoughts. She wanted to hurt him. Angry tears stung her eyes.

"But you shall not take beer away from me! I won't drink beer in your home. But you can't make me stop drinking it elsewhere." She was shouting at him. Her body was trembling in rage. Joseph stood quietly, watching her. When he spoke his voice trembled only slightly.

"You're right. You didn't choose to be my wife. Perhaps I have required too much of you. Forgive me." Joseph turned and left the room. Asenath fell upon the bed in tears of self pity.

When Asenath rose late the next morning Joseph had already gone to his work as vizier. She slipped quickly to her secret chapel and fell on her face before Isis.

"What can I do!" she implored. "Why did you let this happen to me? Why didn't you stop this marriage?" Asenath lay on the ground sobbing, waiting for an answer that did not come.

When Joseph came home at noon, Asenath had been washed and her makeup had been applied. She stood tranquilly at the door as he entered. A quiet fear lurked in her heart to face him.

Joseph wore a strangely sad expression. He greeted her with a strained smile and took her hands. She braced herself for his words, unsure how she would react. But what he had to say was totally unexpected.

"Asenath," Joseph said sadly. "Your grandfather, Ipitoket, has died. He never made it back to On."

CHAPTER 3

"Let thy fountain be blessed: and rejoice with the wife of thy youth." Proverbs 5:18

Forty days the family of Ipitoket mourned his death while his body was prepared by embalming. Asenath went to stay with her parents so that she could properly lament his death.

She saw him before the embalmers began their task. "Oh, Pippa!" she cried, falling against his body. But the warm softness had gone from her grandfather with his loving soul. Nofret reached comforting arms to lead her away.

Joseph would not come until time for the funeral. It was the height of the planting season and he had much to oversee. So, in the home of her parents, Asenath dressed as she should, as a young woman of Egypt. Asenath wept and mourned with her parents, imbibing as much of the cool, pungent beer as she wished.

"I will be part of the funerary priesthood," Nikansut told her proudly.

"I'm glad for you, Niki." She knew that her brother had struggled hard to reach his present plane in the priesthood. It was a great honor to be a part of her grandfather's funeral.

Servants waved large palm fans as Asenath and Nofret sipped beer. "Did your husband have a chapel built for your Isis?" Nofret asked.

"Oh, no!" Asenath answered, sitting up straight. "He doesn't know that I have an Isis. He would only take her away from me. I have carefully hidden her, and he doesn't know that I pray to her."

Nofret clucked her tongue, shaking her head. "It's a shame that the daughter of the priest of the sun should not be allowed a chapel. Shall I have masons sent to build you one?"

31

"No! Joseph wouldn't allow it. I have fashioned a small chapel for her from a shard of pottery. Joseph must not know."

"Then I shall send masons to build a very small chapel, in your hiding place, about which Zaphnath need not know."

Ihat sought Asenath when she sat alone in the roof garden. She sat in her habitual manner at Asenath's feet, resting her arms on her sister's lap. She was silent for several moments, staring away into the horizon.

"The vizier is very handsome," Ihat finally said. "Are you very happy being his wife?" Her large black eyes searched Asenath's face.

"Yes, Ihat, he is handsome. You have always seen him with his wig, but I especially favor his hair, which is golden like the desert sand."

"And are you happy?"

Asenath bit her lip. "He is good to me."

"He makes you dress like Mama, doesn't he?"

Asenath looked at her little sister. Yes, and he won't let me have a chapel to Isis or drink beer in our house, she thought. But she smiled at her sister and tugged her long black braid. "I am a married woman, now, and I must do as my husband desires."

Ihat squinted at her. "But you don't look happy."

"Pippa is gone. I'm not happy about that," Asenath told her.

When Joseph arrived at On Asenath felt strange to be with him again, for they had been apart longer than they had been together. She was sure to wear one of her new dresses.

Early on the morning of the funerary rites, forty-two priests assembled on the shore of the sacred lake, a depository of the inundation of the Nile that was fed by a small channel from the river. Potiphera, high priest of On, was among them, as was Nikansut. Those priests which had been initiated into the Mysteries of Egypt each wore a triangular apron over their kilts.

Joseph and Asenath stood with her family and watched as

judgment was passed by the priests upon the departed soul of the mummy, according to deeds done in his body. Ipitoket was judged worthy by unanimous approval.

His body was then put into a boat. The costumed boatman represented the spirit of death, who would convey the body of the justified dead to its last resting place. He symbolized the boatman of that spiritual boat which would convey the spirit of Ipitoket to the sun, Ra, and at the sun's setting, to the underworld.

The tau cross was laid on the breast of the dead, and the final farewells were said. Then the coffin was closed and sealed. The boatman poled the reed boat along the lake shore to the channel and out into the river.

The forty-two priests and remaining funerary company travelled in boats upriver to the Giza Necropolis, the burial ground of dignitaries. The Royal Necropolis was overlooked by the great Sphinx and guarded by several pyramids. A channel penetrated the Necropolis, and the boats wended their way slowly to the burial site.

During the forty days of embalming a burial chamber had been carved into the solid rock floor of the Necropolis. The coffin of Ipitoket was carried by priests from the channel to the burial chamber, and there it was sealed in stone.

Stone masons had been hired who would erect a stone mastaba, or tomb chapel, above ground. It would be a small structure with a blue ceiling covered with stars like the great chamber in the temple pyramid. A central niche would hold a life sized image of Ipitoket wearing his triangular apron of the priesthood. Before the image would be a small altar for offerings by the family. The priests of Gizah would see that daily offerings were made as well. Half life sized images of Ipitoket's family members would line the walls. The remaining walls and two large square pillars would be covered with relief carvings of scenes from Ipitoket's life. Everything would be painted in bright, cheerful colors. After the burial, seventy days of mourning would be observed. Asenath's family would take daily excursions the few miles from On to Gizah to mourn and make offerings at the mastaba.

Joseph needed to return to Memphis, but agreed to go one last time with Asenath to her grandfather's tomb. In preparation she took black mud from the river's edge in a clay pot. At the nearly built mastaba, as she knelt before the altar on which she had placed her offering, Asenath smeared her face and limbs with the black mud, weeping hysterically.

Joseph did not interfere with her grieving, but when she had finished, he took her hand and walked away from the tomb. They walked silently for a few minutes, stepping between mastabas, some ancient, some new. Finally Joseph spoke.

"What is the purpose of bringing an offering to your grandfather's tomb? And why do you weep so?"

Asenath stopped walking and looked curiously into his eyes. "The offerings are for my grandfather to consume in the underworld. I weep because my grandfather is dead. I believe that his soul is in the underworld with the great god Osiris, keeper of the dead. But I weep because I no longer can see him and speak with him." She paused. "I miss my grandfather."

Joseph reached and pulled her against him, and she relaxed and laid her head against his chest. He rubbed her shoulders and back, laying his clean shaven face against her neck. Suddenly the fountain opened and she wept, not the tears of mourning that she had shed at the tomb, but great cleansing sobs for her lost grandfather, for herself.

When her tears had subsided, she and Joseph surveyed the pyramids, whose polished marble sides gleamed in the sun.

"These are the tombs of kings," Asenath told him. "All the graves are guarded by the Sphinx and the Great Pyramid. The Great Pyramid isn't a tomb, but a temple," she explained. "Only those who are initiated into the Mysteries may go there."

"The Mysteries?" Joseph asked.

They sat in the shadow of a mastaba looking at the Great

Pyramid, which towered above all else.

"My people worship and revere many gods," Asenath said. Joseph nodded. "But the priesthood doesn't, really. They, too, do homage to many gods, but they worship the sun god, Ra, and his siblings. The goddess Nut is the mother of Ra, the sun. When she gave birth to his brother, Osiris, a voice sounded throughout the world, saying, 'The lord of all the earth is born.' Nut also gave birth to Isis and Typhon."

"When Osiris was grown he became the King of Egypt. His brother Typhon had ambition to usurp the throne. Isis, the sister of Osiris, and also his wife, found out. Typhon tricked Osiris into a box, clamped it closed with nails, and poured melted lead over all the cracks and crevices. He cast it into the Nile River where it meets the sea."

"Isis put on the mourning apparel of widowhood and searched Egypt for her husband's body. She found the chest at the coast of Byblos, lodged in the branches of a tamarisk bush which grew around and concealed the box. Isis took the box to a desert place, where she performed magical rites which temporarily animated Osiris. Isis was able to conceive her son, Horus. Isis hid the box and departed. But Typhon found it and tore the body of Osiris into fourteen parts and scattered them about Egypt."

"And these are your gods?" Joseph asked.

"Yes. Isis was able to find all the parts of his body but the phallus, which had been eaten by fish. This is why the priests do not eat fish. The obelisks of Egypt represent the lost phallus of Osiris. Isis gave him a golden phallus and performed ceremonies necessary to insure the life of Osiris in the underworld. Isis and her son Horus are referred to as the Widow and her Son."

"Osiris is the god of the underworld and the judge of the dead. He embodies the secret and sacred wisdom reserved for the priesthood, who are proficient in secret rites. Osiris signifies the divine at-one-ment with the Absolute, the end of all illumination. By his life, death, and resurrection, he reveals the means by which the mortal consciousness can be at one, too."

"Isis is the Mother of the Mysteries, the Queen of Heaven. I venerate Isis, the mourning widow, and her son Horus. The Pharaoh is the embodiment of Horus on earth, the divine image, and the priesthood are the Hori to avenge the destruction of wisdom and restore the reign of Osiris."

"This is what I believe, Joseph. It is why I desire to have a chapel to the goddess Isis, and why I long to bring daily offerings to her." Asenath watched him. Would he understand and relent?

Joseph's eyes took on a faraway look. "My Great-grandfather, Abraham, lived in Ur of the Chaldees. His people worshipped gods symbolized by idols. But Jehovah, Creator of Heaven and earth, called Abraham out from his people to father a people dedicated to Him. He made great and wondrous promises to Abraham, to bless the whole earth through his seed. These promises were repeated to my grandfather, Isaac."[6]

"When my father, Jacob, met God face to face, his name was changed to Israel."[7] Joseph paused at mention of his father. His voice softened. "I loved my father dearly. But my brothers hated me, at least the elder ten."

"You have ten brothers?" Asenath asked him incredulously.

"I have ten older brothers and one younger." Joseph's voice broke, and his shoulders trembled. "The younger, Benjamin," he continued with difficulty, "is the son of my mother. The other ten have other mothers."

Asenath sensed his anguish and took his hand in both of hers. He smiled through the tears that had filled his eyes.

"It was my ten older brothers who sold me as a slave."

---

[6] Genesis 22:17,18; 26:24

[7] Genesis 32:28,30

"Your brothers?"

"They first planned to kill me, but instead sold me to a caravan of Ishmaelites travelling to Egypt."[8]

"How awful!" Asenath breathed.

Joseph squeezed her hands and smiled again. "My brothers meant it for evil. But my God is greater than any evil, and He meant it for good."

"Isn't He also the God of your brothers?"

"The Lord is sovereign God over all, but He is the Lord of those who put their trust in Him."

"Our religions are very different," Asenath said.

"Yes," he agreed. They sat at the edge of the arid land and watched the sun paint the shadows of the pyramids long.

After the evening meal Potiphera asked Joseph to walk with him. "I would like you to see the Temple of Ra," he said. Joseph reached a hand to Asenath and she accompanied him. They walked through the cool dusk to the wall surrounding the temple. Before the temple stood a large, tall obelisk covered with the symbols of Egypt. A tall gate, with palace facade, opened to an inner court which surrounded the temple. Lamps on poles burned brightly in the night and illuminated their approach to the temple door.

Following a long, narrow corridor, they came to the interior of the temple of the sun god, which was dimly lit. Lesser priests attended the lamps at night. Large round columns, all intricately adorned with carvings and brightly painted, lined the walls of the large, high ceilinged room. They looked up and saw the star studded blue ceiling above them. Doorways led to many rooms off the main sanctuary. The far end of the room was the abode of the huge idol of Ra, the sun god. All about him lamps burned, and before him on the large altar lay offerings of food and flowers. The offerings were the property of the priests who

---

[8] Genesis 37:27

attended Ra. They glided silently about their duties, retrieving the offerings and cleaning the altar and floor.

"As high priest I do none of the menial tasks," Potiphera explained to his son in law. "However, it falls to me once every thirteen days to attend the image personally. He is cleansed and dressed in the morning. Food offerings are given to him three times daily. In the evening he is cleansed again."

"He has eyes," Joseph observed, "but does he see you? He has ears, but does he hear?"

"It is not the image, Zaphnath, but the spirit behind the image to which I pray and yield devotion. The image is the visible symbol of the invisible spirit."

They walked out of the temple into the lamplight. Potiphera put his hand on Joseph's arm, and they stopped walking. "Zaphnath, you are vizier of Egypt. We are a good people. We have a good way of life, and a good religion. You should try to become one of us."

"My people do not shave their beards. I shave every day, as the Egyptians," Joseph told him. "I dress in the kilt of the Egyptians. I wear a thick wool wig." Joseph reached up and scratched his head. "I do not require your daughter to eat fish or vegetables, and we have no wine, as she requested as the daughter of a priest. I try, sir, to live as an Egyptian." Joseph paused and took a deep breath.

"But I can't worship the gods of Egypt. Whatever they are, image or spirit, I can't worship them. I worship Jehovah, the Maker of all. My heart, my love, belong to the Lord. Neither can I partake of those elements of Egypt that oppose my God. My God is my life."

Potiphera nodded and resumed walking toward home. "It is understandable. Perhaps in time you will find our gods acceptable."

Joseph pulled his wig from his head and sat on the bed beside Asenath. His sand colored hair had grown and now fell in soft waves against his head. Asenath loved his hair. She reached a hand to stroke his locks and he caught her hand, putting it to his lips.

"Was ever a stranger marriage made than ours?" he asked her.

She did not reply.

"I am second in the kingdom of Egypt; only Pharaoh is higher than I. All Egypt looks to me to do the right thing, so that they may live through the prophesied famine. And they pray to their gods and their ancestors." His aqua eyes consumed her. "But their vizier trusts in the Lord God alone. The religion of Egypt rules their very lives." He added softly, "It rules yours as well. But I do not live by the religion of Egypt. You are the daughter of the priest of the sun god! And you are my wife. Was ever a stranger marriage made?" he asked again.

In the morning Joseph prepared for his return to Memphis. The days of mourning for her grandfather were not completed, but Asenath caught his hand before he departed their bedroom.

"I wish to return with you, today," she said.

Joseph smiled. Lifting his brows he said, "The days of mourning are unfinished."

"But I wish to be with you." She looked shyly away and said, "I missed you when we were apart."

"But I'm the one who forbids you beer and who makes you dress as an old woman," he said with a tease.

"And you are the father of my child," Asenath said softly.

Joseph sobered suddenly. He took her hands. Wonder lit his handsome face and beautiful eyes.

"You are with child?" he asked.

"Yes."

"Praise be to the Lord God!"

CHAPTER 4

"Thy wife shall be as a fruitful vine by the sides of thine house: thy children like olive plants round about thy table."
Psalms 128:3

A servant waved a large palm frond above Asenath's head as she sat in the shade of the large brick storage silo. Joseph stood on the ramp which spiraled to the top edge of the silo and directed the builders. Stacks of straw mud bricks were rolled up the incline in small wagons. Masons stacked the bricks and sealed them together with mortar from buckets. The crops were growing beneath the Egyptian sun, watered generously with the intricate irrigation system that carried the precious liquid from the Nile River. Joseph was in charge of the building of bins to store the excess grains. The mortar dried hard and sure in the hot sun. The men, too, cooked brown beneath the searing orb. At regular intervals a halt was called, and servants bearing jugs of cool water went about and dipped out drinks to the working men. Asenath watched Joseph speak to the workers as he passed them while descending the ramp. Smiles lit many of the weary faces at his words. She watched him pat the back of one man in encouragement, and she was touched.

Unaccustomed as she was with taskmasters and their laborers, she was sure that Joseph's consideration of his men was unusual. When the sun had reached its zenith the men descended the incline to rest in the scant shade of the growing tower. Young girls scurried to serve them cool water and bread and fruits from trays.

Joseph sat beside his wife and they were served the noon meal. Asenath had missed his customary returns home at noontime while he oversaw the building of the silos. When she had asked to accompany him that morning his eyes had glowed and his face flushed in pleasure.

Joseph reclined against the brick wall and bit a grape from a bunch that he held aloft. He chewed it slowly, watching Asenath as she ate. Her face blushed with the heat, which bothered her more now that her body began to swell with child.

"When these storage bins are completed, I must leave for Avis to build bins there," he told her. She looked quickly into his aqua eyes.

"I shall accompany you," she said.

Joseph took her hand. "It will not be easy, there. Apepi told me that I must sleep in a tent. I don't think it would be comfortable for you. The servants will be with you at our home, and I will finish the task as quickly as I can."

Asenath's mouth pouted. "Why must Egypt's vizier sleep in a tent?" she asked.

"The grain silos will be built near the fields, but away from the city." Joseph paused. "A tent is more familiar to me than a home of bricks."

She bit into a slice of melon, but her eyes asked for explanation.

"I was born in a tent and slept in tents for seventeen years, until I was brought to Egypt as a slave."

"Why didn't your father build a structure of stone?"

"My family grazes sheep and cattle, and therefore moves from pasture land to pasture land. A tent is the only practical home for wandering nomads."

"Will you like your tent, then, better than our home?" she asked him with a tease. But her heart was truly wondering.

Joseph smiled and shook his head. "No," he said simply.

When Joseph left for Avis Asenath was vexed. Each day lay like a burden upon her. The masons from her mother came and constructed a tiny, yet sufficient chapel for Isis. That was a consolation to Asenath, and for two days occupied her mind. But the irritation returned, so she ordered a boat to On.

Because of her condition Asenath wore the clothing

Joseph had ordered, even while at her father's house. She and her mother made a daily trip upriver to the Necropolis at Giza to place offerings at Ipitoket's tomb. They smeared the black Nile mud upon limbs and faces, and wept the sorrowful tears of mourning, to make up for Asenath's absence during the proper days of mourning.

When they returned to On, they were bathed by servants and their makeup was refreshed. Then they sat in the shady garden attended by servants waving palm fronds, and drank cool beer. Asenath could not seem to get enough of the pungent liquid, and revelled in the lightheaded serenity it afforded.

Each morning Asenath and Nofret worked their devotions in the proper chapel of Potiphera's home. Asenath thanked Nofret for the tiny chapel which had been built at her own home, but she did enjoy proper veneration of Isis. She joyed to pour the dark, dank beer out before her goddess, acutely aware that Isis must be pleased.

"Queen of Heaven," she implored before the large idol in her father's chapel, "keep Zaphnathpaaneah in safety at Avis." She always used Apepi's name for Joseph in her petitions to Isis, so as not to confuse the goddess. "Watch over this child," she added, touching her swelling abdomen. "And let him be a man child."

Asenath often visited Potiphera in the temple. She sometimes watched the daily sacrifice of a goat before the idol, as her father read the omens in the slaughtered beast's entrails and organs. Pride welled up in her breast that her father was a man of such importance in Egypt.

Nikansut was busy learning the business of the Temple and preparing for his own initiation into the Mysteries, which he hoped to soon commence. Asenath found him sitting beneath a lamp late one night. She sat at his side and watched as he carefully marked a small soft clay tablet with his wedge shaped tool. He was copying the inscriptions from an ancient clay shard, carefully duplicating the stilted figures as well.

"You do very well, Niki," she told him, admiring his work. "I didn't know you could do that."

Nikansut smiled at her. "I went to school."

"Everyone I know went to school," she replied, "but not many can copy like that."

"I enjoy it. And ciphering, too. I could sit for hours and add up figures." Nikansut pursed his lips. "Papa thinks it's a great waste of my time. Soon I'll be involved in my initiation and won't have time for this anymore. So I do it while I can."

Asenath found that she avoided being alone with Ihat, because she feared the question she always asked, "Are you happy?"

As much as she loved her family, and although Joseph was not there, something seemed to call Asenath back to Memphis. She kissed her family fondly and returned to her empty house. Servants swarmed about her, but without Joseph the elegant rooms were barren.

To alleviate her boredom, Asenath walked through the streets of her glorious city, accompanied by two female servants and two males. She did her worship at the temples and visited many of the little shops that dotted the streets.

She stopped before a shop sporting jewelry to listen to the bartering of a young woman patron. The woman, who was richly jewelled and attended by servants, was haughtily surveying a bracelet.

"It is four ontoons, madame," the harried merchant affirmed.

"You are a thief," the woman said evenly and calmly, hanging the bracelet back onto the proper hook.

"Three ontoons," the merchant quoted quickly.

The woman eyed him for a moment and plucked the bracelet off the rack. "Pay him," she ordered a servant, while she slid the band of jewelled gold up her arm. She examined it with a frown and then moved along the street.

In the crush of passersby and each with a large entourage,

the two women met mid step, unable to pass each other. Asenath knew she stared, but something drew her to this woman. The other laughed aloud at their predicament and reached her hand to Asenath.

"It seems we are destined to meet, here on the street. I am Nophtet, wife of the Venerable Jash." She smiled, and Asenath was warmed and felt instantly at ease with her.

"I am Asenath, wife of Zaphnathpaaneah, vizier of Egypt."

Nophtet was instantly on her knees on the hard pavement before Asenath. Her servants followed suit. The color rose quickly to Asenath's face, and she reached to pull Nophtet to her feet, catching her breath as she bent over.

"No, please," she appealed. "Do not. It is my husband who is vizier, not I."

Nophtet and her servants rose to their feet, and Nophtet smiled. "Since the gods have brought us together so, will you come with me to my home, and allow me the honor of entertaining you there?"

"I would love to come. Joseph is at Avis, and I've been quite lonely."

Nophtet's home was near the palace of Apepi. Her husband, the Venerable Jash, was high counsellor of the king. Asenath relaxed in the cool shade sipping beer and listening to Nophtet's friendly chatter. The delicious knowledge that she had met a friend washed over her as she warmed with the beer.

"When will the child come?" Nophtet asked.

"In the midst of the inundation," Asenath told her.

"Is it the vizier's child?"

"Yes, of course," Asenath answered, alarmed.

Nophtet's musical laughter floated around her. "Yes, of course," she mocked gently. "And how do you know the child does not belong to Joseph, the one you miss so?"

Asenath held her goblet of beer midair in puzzlement. She wrinkled her brow and blinked her eyes to clear her thoughts. Slowly she understood her friend's confusion and laughed lightly.

"Oh, I see. Joseph is my husband's name. Zaphnathpaaneah is the name given him by Apepi."

"So it's your husband you miss."

"Yes."

Nophtet tapped her lips in thought with a slender finger. "That's quite curious. Nice, but curious. You see, dear, I would never miss the Venerable Jash. He's at least twenty years my senior. My position as his wife affords me comforts and riches. But love? No, I have a paramour for that."

Asenath was silent, unsure what she could reply. So she said, "I think I could learn to love Joseph. But he can't love me."

Nophtet's curiosity was instantly aroused. She leaned closer to Asenath. "And why is that, dear?" she asked softly.

Asenath looked away from Nophtet's intense gaze. "My husband's very life is his God. He doesn't venerate any of the gods of Egypt. His God is from his country." She paused, unsure how to explain Joseph's God, for she herself did not fully understand.

"He will not allow me a chapel to Isis." She looked at Nophtet. "He will not allow me to drink beer." At these words Nophtet signalled a servant to replenish Asenath's drink. Asenath sensed that she had a sympathetic listener, and she warmed to the sad tale of her woes.

"He would not allow me to dress as a young woman, even before this," she gestured toward her expanding figure. "And we must observe his religious rituals. We do nothing, no work at all, not even the servants, on each seventh day."

Nophtet was clucking her tongue and shaking her head sadly at Asenath's recitation.

"Well, I can certainly understand why you wouldn't love him," Nophtet declared. "But why shouldn't he love you? It sounds to me as if you do everything you can to please him."

The tears came then, and Asenath was unable to restrain

them. They came in torrents, and she cried through her tears, nodding her head furiously, "Yes! I do!" Nophtet dismissed the servants from the room. When Asenath had calmed a little she looked at Nophtet through her smudged makeup and said, "Joseph loves his God. He can't truly love me, because I worship Isis."

Nophtet gathered the trembling form into her arms and soothed her. "What a shame," she crooned, "for a man to pass up such love as you could give him for a god! What matters it what god one venerates? It matters not at all!" She rocked Asenath back and forth gently.

When Asenath was finally able to sit calmly and sip her beer, Nophtet spoke confidentially to her. "This will have to pass first, of course," she said, indicating Asenath's swollen belly. "But when you once more have your figure, my advice to you, dear friend, is to forget your husband. Somewhere in the ranks of gorgeous men living in Memphis there is a man who can truly worship you as you deserve. Find him, but mind you, be discrete, for the vizier's position affords you comfort and wealth. But find love elsewhere, dear. You deserve it."

When Asenath was once again in her own home, she sat stroking Roke's sleek coat and pondered the counsel of her new friend. No, she did not desire a lover. She only desired for Joseph to love her. And that, she knew, could never be, for Joseph would never change. His God would always be his life.

Asenath visited Nophtet again, and Nophtet came with a train of servants to Asenath's home. Having a friend with which to talk helped the hours to pass, and one evening a messenger bore news that Joseph would return on the morrow.

Asenath oversaw a thorough cleaning of the large house and preparation of a grand meal. She stood nervously on the balcony which ran the width of her house and watched for him. At last he came, quietly greeting the servant who let him in at the gate. Asenath's heart raced as she watched him approach the house. He lifted his eyes to her and waved. She waved back, while the tension in her stomach almost made her sick.

Joseph took the stairs two at a time and stood before her. He smiled broadly.

"Hello, welcome," Asenath said awkwardly. She felt suddenly a stranger before the grand man standing before her.

"Hello," the vizier of Egypt said, bowing before her. Taking her hand in his he brought it to his lips. Together they went inside to the meal awaiting them.

Asenath accompanied Joseph to a dinner given by Apepi. The king gave her a seat of honor at his side, while he talked about her coming child. His green eyes danced in amusement at her discomfort. He was no stranger to expectant women, for he had a dozen children.

Asenath had attended many dinners of state, both in the palace and elsewhere. But for a reason she could not perceive, she felt uncomfortable when the troupe of naked dancers swayed their provocative dance before the pharaoh, almost touching Joseph in their gyrations. Perhaps it was because her own body was anything but alluring as she carried her child. She knew that Joseph avoided the dancers purposely with his eyes. She couldn't explain her husbands oddity, but she was glad of it.

When the dancers had gone and quiet music attended the meal, Pharaoh Apepi turned to his vizier with a broad smile.

"Zaphnathpaaneah," he said, slowly pronouncing the name he had given. "I am well pleased with your service to Egypt. I have recommended you to your father in law," Apepi nodded toward Asenath, "for the Mysteries. The coming inundation is an excellent time to begin the rituals."

Joseph bowed his head before the king, then looked him in the eye. "Thank you, great Apepi, for your praise and your confidence. My wife has explained to me some of the magnitude of the Mysteries. I respect my father in law, and you, sir." Joseph bowed his head again. "But I understand that the Mysteries are coupled with veneration of your gods. You understand, great Apepi, that I reverence only the God of

Heaven, Creator of Heaven and earth. I worship Him only. I can serve Him only. I thank you profoundly, sir, for your offer. But I must decline."

Apepi watched his vizier earnestly. Then his green eyes sparkled and he smiled as he clapped Joseph on the back. "I will not press you, Zaphnathpaaneah. Your God gave you the interpretation to my dreams. I won't force you to dishonor Him."

Asenath noted Potiphar and Hoptet among the guests at Apepi's dinner. They smiled at her when she caught their eye, but she noted the fear still written on their faces as they peered at her illustrious husband.

Joseph was especially busy as the last of the crops were harvested and the excess stored away in the brick silos. Truly it had been a bounteous harvest. Had it indeed been caused by Joseph's God? Asenath wondered. Did the gods of Egypt have nothing to do with the blessing of plentiful yield?

At last the fields were bared and the overflow of the Nile began. As monsoon rains emptied into the southern Nile, the waters swelled and spilled over onto the rich farm lands of Egypt, carrying with them rich nutrients to deposit along the river and on the delta.

And Joseph was home. He would go no more to the fields or storage silos until the waters had abated and planting began again. Apepi sent an invitation for a banquet of his court, and Joseph went alone, for Asenath was heavy with child, and in much discomfort.

Asenath waddled down the stairs and across the broad lawn to the far side of the pond, where she knelt awkwardly before her goddess.

"Oh Queen of Heaven," she implored, as she had since becoming pregnant, "let this child be a son. Perhaps then my husband will truly love me." As she knelt thus a strong spasm seized her, causing her to catch and hold her breath. When it had passed she straightened herself and stood, kneading her belly with her hands.

She left her tiny chapel and walked beside the manmade pond, watching the reflection of the sunset in the smooth waters. She was suddenly arrested as another squeezing cramp engulfed her, this time leaving her frightened.

Asenath hurried clumsily up her steps and called Zedek in alarm. He bowed before her as another pain swept her body. When it was over she commanded him to send immediately for the midwife.

"Shall I send for the master?" he asked.

Asenath was unsure whether a man should be involved in the birth of his child, but said, "Yes."

Pacing the floor, Asenath suffered through each onslaught of pain gripping a chair or a window ledge. Footsteps on the stairs brought a sigh from Asenath, for the midwife might know how to ease the pain. But it was Joseph who burst through the doorway. Upon seeing him Asenath broke into tears of disappointment. She wanted the midwife just now, not a man. What could a man do for her?

Joseph approached her anxiously, attempting to take her into his arms, but she pushed him away. He stood back, shaken. She caught one brief glimpse of his sea blue eyes and saw great concern there. But the midwife entered with a servant bearing the birthing stool, and Joseph was ushered away.

The midwife checked her progress and shook her head. "It will be awhile, my dear."

Asenath felt suddenly ashamed before the older woman. "Forgive me for calling you so soon," she said. "I didn't know."

The woman smiled and patted Asenath's hand. "First mother's often call me early. It's alright. We will get you a good, healthy child."

A labour pain gripped Asenath and she groaned loudly. The midwife showed her how to breathe the pain away as a servant woman bathed her brow with a cool cloth. The hours passed, and with them the pain became so intense that Asenath feared that she would die. Between the searing pains she thought of death, and wondered what would be her fate. Grave doubts rose in her heart. Would she live beyond the tomb?

But she did not die. Just before the sun rose Asenath gave birth to a son. The servant woman took the wailing infant and cleansed him. She then rubbed his small body with salt and wrapped him tightly. When Asenath and the room had been cleaned the midwife and her servant left wearily.

Asenath lay in bed with the infant at her breast. His first frenzied attempts to nurse had tired him, and he slept. Joseph entered and knelt at her side. He did not wear his wig, and he had not been shaved. Asenath, exhausted from her night of toil, noticed Joseph's weary expression and realized that he had spent a sleepless night as well.

Joseph smiled and reached to stroke the baby's soft cheek. He lifted the fragile fingers in his own and the tiny hand grasped his.

"I give him the name Manasseh," Joseph said softly. "God has made me forget all my toil and my father's house."[9]

"I prayed to Isis for a son," Asenath breathed.

Joseph's expression changed and he looked at her sadly. He let go his son's hand and stood. Fear clutched her heart. But it was the truth! She had prayed for a son.

Joseph's voice was low and choked with emotion as he spoke. "The Lord God of Heaven and earth is the Creator of all life, Asenath. It is He, and He alone, Who gave us our son."

Their eyes locked, each unwavering, neither yielding. Finally Asenath turned her eyes away. She heard Joseph depart, and she dissolved into tears.

Potiphera and Nofret arrived that evening. The children had not come, for Asenath didn't need so much excitement on her first day as a mother. After admiring their grandson with much

---

[9] Genesis 41:51

praise, they went to the home of Potiphar to stay the night.

When Manasseh was five days old Nikansut, Ihat, Ipi, and Wehemki came to see their nephew. Asenath felt stronger each day, and enjoyed giving her every moment and attention to her baby. Joseph had slept in another room since the birth of their son, and Asenath felt a strange breach between them.

When Manasseh was eight days old, Joseph came to the bedroom and lifted the child from his small bed. Asenath followed him as he went to the dining room and sat on a chair. On a tray at his side were a knife, a bowl of water, and a strip of white linen.

Asenath sat at Joseph's side and reached a hand to grasp his arm.

"Joseph," she said in alarm. "What are you going to do?"

He looked kindly at her. There was no trace of anger or annoyance. "When the Lord God called my great grandfather, Abraham, from his country and his people, He made a covenant with him and his descendants. This that I do is the sign of that covenant between the Lord and me, between the Lord and Manasseh."

"What is the sign? What are you going to do to him?" Fear edged into her voice.

"I will circumcise Manasseh as a sign that he is one of God's chosen ones, a descendant of Abraham."[10] Joseph looked intently at Asenath. "It must be done. It will not be pleasant to watch, so you don't have to. But if you stay, you must not interfere. It must be done." He paused. "Do you understand?"

"What do you mean? What is circumcise?"

Joseph explained briefly, and her face blanched.

"No! I won't let you do that to my baby!"

"I was circumcised as an infant, as was my father. The pain will be brief and quickly forgotten. It must be done. The

---

[10] Genesis 17:9-12

Lord God has commanded it."

Asenath searched his face. He was serious. She knew that she was helpless to stop him. She stood and quietly said, "When you're done he will need me to comfort him. I will wait in the bedroom."

Asenath plugged her ears tightly and tried not to hear the tiny baby's shriek of pain as he was circumcised. In just a moment Joseph handed Manasseh to her and she soothed away his tears.

When the baby was quietly nursing, Asenath turned her eyes, burning with fury, to her husband. "Your God requires barbaric rituals," she said harshly.

Joseph nodded slowly. "It may seem barbaric," he said, "but Manasseh won't remember this day. The sign in his body will always remind him, though, that he belongs to the Lord God of Heaven."

"He is Egyptian, too, Joseph," she said less harshly, stroking the moist hair above the baby's ear.

"Yes, he is Egyptian, too," Joseph agreed. "But the Lord God of Heaven is his God."

****

Asenath hurried to keep up with Joseph's long strides through the market street. He noticed her lagging and slowed. At the shop of the wig maker, Joseph stopped and entered.

Upon seeing the vizier, all in the shop knelt low. Joseph spoke a word to discontinue their veneration and turned to the wig maker.

"I need a male lamb of the first year. Could I purchase one from you?"

"Your eminence," the man said, "my sheep are kept in Goshen, where the grazing lands are. I could have one sent for. Would two days be soon enough?"

"Yes. Please have it delivered to my house."

The man bowed again, and they departed the shop. Joseph took Manasseh into his arms and Asenath followed through the crowded streets to the home of Potiphar.

It was only their second visit to the home of Potiphar. Servants escorted them to the living quarters, where Hoptet and Potiphar sat. As they entered the room Potiphar and his wife were instantly on their faces before Joseph.

"Please rise," Joseph told them as he and Asenath were seated.

Potiphar rose slowly, pulling Hoptet up beside him. They quickly seated themselves and Potiphar motioned for refreshment. Joseph shook his head and waved it away.

"In two days I will do sacrifice to the Lord God. I have come to ask your forgiveness."

Potiphar and Hoptet exchanged questioning glances. Potiphar cleared his throat and spoke.

"My wife told me, since your last visit to our home, the truth of what happened those many years ago," Potiphar said. He looked beseechingly at Joseph. "We truly beg your forgiveness, Great One." He paused. "But for what have we to forgive you?" he asked.

"You have lived in fear since the Lord God made me vizier of Egypt. Do not fear. I hold no grudge against you, or your wife. Forgive my..." Joseph paused, searching for words. "Forgive my eminence which frightens you. I have forgiven all."

The man and his wife were suddenly on their faces once more before Joseph, both weeping openly.

"Why do you forgive such a trespass?" Potiphar asked.

Joseph placed a hand on the shoulder of each. "I forgive you in the name of the Lord God, Creator of heaven and earth. I can bear you no ill."

They walked along silently toward their home, except for the cooing of Manasseh. As they entered their courtyard Asenath stopped.

"Joseph," she said. He turned to her.

"For such a crime you could put them both into the prison in which you suffered so many years."

"Yes, I could."

"Then why forgive? You need not show them deference because they are friends to my parents."

"As I told them, Asenath, I forgave them in the name of the Lord God. He has blessed me so richly." Joseph's blue-green eyes smiled into hers. "He gave me you, and Manasseh. And when I do sacrifice to Him, I can bear ill toward no man."

"What sacrifice?"

"You will accompany me, as will Manasseh. You will see."

Fear clutched Asenath's heart. She did not know all the strange requirements of Joseph's God. She feared to learn them, especially since her infant son must be there, too. Since the circumcision of Manasseh, Asenath did not fully trust her husband or his God's demands.

CHAPTER 5

"Every wise woman buildeth her house: but the foolish plucketh it down with her hands." Proverbs 14:1

Joseph had carefully examined the bleating lamb. "It must be perfect," he told Asenath. Zedek was commissioned to carry the unhappy animal as Joseph led his family away from the city into a desert place.

There Joseph collected stones and piled them in a ragged heap. On top of the stones he laid sticks of wood which had been carried by a servant. When his preparations were complete, he gestured for Asenath to come nearer. She shifted Manasseh's weight in her arms and approached hesitantly.

Joseph took the lamb from Zedek and knelt on the ground beside it. It squirmed and tried to escape, but he held it firmly.

"When the first man, Adam, and his wife, Eve, sinned and disobeyed the Lord God, He made a way to reconcile them to Himself," Joseph explained. "He promised to them that Messiah would someday give His life for their sins. And as a token, the Lord shed the blood of a lamb, and clothed the man and his wife with the skin.[11] Because I love and trust the God of Heaven and earth, the Creator of all, I will shed the blood of this lamb." Asenath shuddered. "This lamb will bear the punishment for my sins, as Messiah will someday bear the sins of the world."

Joseph bowed his head in silence as he held the struggling lamb.

"What sins?" Asenath asked him.

He looked up at her for a moment in silence. "Every thought that I have, every word that I speak, and every deed that

---

[11] Genesis 3

I do, that does not please my Lord."

"You live your life to please your God. What have you ever done against Him?"

Joseph looked at her again silently. She saw a tear glisten in his eye as he spoke. "My heart rebels that I am here in Egypt and not at home with my father's family. I often question my Lord in my heart. My every thought is not submitted to Him." He swallowed with the strain of his confession. "And I often lose my temper."

"With me?"

He only nodded.

"Then your God must hate me. For I don't even worship Him. I think thoughts so wicked you couldn't imagine them. I don't live my life for your God at all."

The tears slid along Joseph's nose and dropped onto the lamb's wool. He nodded his head. "I know that you don't. And it's a sorrow to me, Asenath," he said. "But God doesn't hate you. He loves you."

Asenath snickered at his words.

The blue green sea of Joseph's eyes continued to flow in tears. His muscles bulged to hold the lamb still, but his eyes looked at Asenath with such sorrow that she couldn't bear it. She looked away, and saw that Zedek, too, knelt upon the ground in penitent expression.

"It is the dearest desire of my heart," Joseph told her as she strained to hear his quiet words, "that you will someday love and trust the Lord God."

Asenath did not look at him until she heard the final bleat of the lamb and quickly looked to see its life pour from a slit in its throat into a basin on the ground. It slumped into a heap, which Joseph lifted tenderly and placed on top of the sticks of wood. He slowly poured the blood from the basin onto the lamb and sticks and stones. A servant handed him a small brazier from which he shook hot coals onto the wood. Asenath watched as the sticks caught fire, and soon the whole of Joseph's offering was ablaze. The acrid scent of burning wool and flesh stung her nostrils and she stepped away, but Joseph remained on his knees, praying to his God, until the whole was consumed.

When Joseph's offering to his God was only a smoldering heap of stones, he sat in the shade of a large rock and watched the day wane about him. Asenath joined him, leaning her back against the rock as she nursed her child. They watched the desert animals scurry from the shadows in search of food.

"My mother was a lot like you." Joseph's voice in the stillness startled her, but his words astonished her.

"Like me?"

"She bowed down and prayed to images."

"Your mother?"

"Yes. Her father's family knew the true God of Heaven, but chose to follow the way of the people of the land where they lived. When my mother left her home with my father, she took with her small images of her gods.[12] I saw the images when I was a very small child. But in time I no longer saw them. When my father came face to face with God, he changed. I believe that my mother also changed, and learned to trust in the Lord." Joseph's shoulders shook with emotion. "She died at Benjamin's birth, when I was very young."

"I can't imagine growing up without a mother," Asenath told him softly.

"My father had other wives," Joseph said. "But they were not my mother. I loved my father dearly, and he was very fond of me. He gave me a many colored coat, which caused my older brothers much envy.[13] I think they even hated me because of it. And then I had the dreams."

"What dreams?"

"First I dreamed that my brothers and I were binding

---

[12] Genesis 31:30-34

[13] Genesis 37:3

sheaves of grain in a field. All at once my sheaf stood up alone and my brothers' sheaves bowed down to mine. Then I dreamed that the sun and moon and eleven stars bowed down to me![14] The worse thing was that I told my dreams to my brothers. I guess they hated me all the more. That's why they sold me as a slave. I'm sure my father believes me to be dead. I don't even know if he still lives."

Joseph's shoulders shook again with emotion. Asenath placed her hand on his arm. In one swift motion Joseph gathered her and Manasseh into his arms and wept.

Manasseh was a beautiful child. He had the thick black hair of his mother, but his eyes were the blue of twilight, deep and rich. When he learned to crawl, he went everywhere, pulling things down on him, dumping the large vases of flowers. His nurse chased him to exhaustion, her exhaustion. Asenath, too, constantly retrieved him from danger and trouble. When Joseph returned home each day, Manasseh was instantly placed into his arms.

Joseph loved his son. He taught the tiny boy about his God. He prayed with him. Asenath watched her baby fall in love with his papa, and she was certain that he would someday fall in love with his papa's God.

Asenath had missed the celebration of the festival of Ra while carrying her child. As the festival approached she asked permission of Joseph to take Manasseh to On for the celebration.

Joseph pursed his lips. "I would rather that you wouldn't go. I don't want Manasseh exposed to the veneration of Ra. He must learn to love and trust the true God of Heaven and earth."

Asenath faced him stubbornly with her hands on her hips. "I don't worship your God. I worship the gods of Egypt. Manasseh has a right to know about them, too." She squinted her eyes at the vizier of Egypt. "My father is the priest of the

---

[14] Genesis 37:6-9

Sun God." Her fervor suddenly melted and she dropped her eyes. "Please let me go," she ended softly.

Joseph sighed. "Go," he said simply.

Asenath always loved festival. She bound Manasseh snugly to her back and accompanied her parents to the Temple of Ra in the darkness of early morning. Sturdy wooden ladders had been raised along the south edge of the temple, and servants helped the family mount to the great height safely. There on the flat roof they were seated in places of prominence to await the resurrection of the sun. Behind them a steady stream of sun worshippers climbed the ladders to the roof, crowding together to accommodate as many as possible. Every roof in the city of On held worshippers of the sun.

As the first tinge of pink colored the horizon, a minor priest began the chant. It started low as a moaning wind and grew in volume and intensity with each repetition. Asenath joined the many voices that entered the chant. Worshippers broke into discordant song. When the glowing orange orb lifted a small sliver above the edge of the earth, Potiphera fell on his face prostrate in veneration. Everyone upon the crowded rooftop followed suit, bodies crushing bodies in attempt at prone positions. Asenath prostrated herself beside her father, her infant son silently bowing upon her back. As the radiant disc elevated in full above the horizon, Potiphera raised himself onto his knees and spread his arms toward the sun.

The singing and chanting ceased as the worshippers raised their arms upward. Potiphera's voice rang out through the stillness. "Our great and wondrous god! We your people praise you and adore you. Shine upon us with your golden light. Give life to us, to our beasts and to our fields. We praise you our great and wondrous god!"

Great cheering and exultant joy burst forth from the crowd of worshippers as they leapt to their feet, greeting the sun.

The crowd upon the rooftop made way for the priestly families to pass to the ladders, where they were helped to the ground. A long file of worshippers followed them from the rooftop and from all parts of the city toward the tall obelisk which stood before the sun temple.

Four streamers had been attached to the pointed summit of the obelisk. Four young girls grasped the dangling streamers and began to dance about the tower to rousing music. The worshippers sang and clapped their hands, crowding close to catch a glimpse of the dance. At last the girls had wound the streamers closely to the obelisk, and Potiphera raised his hands. He waited as lesser priests passed the word through the crowd for silence. When quiet came at last Potiphera's voice thundered against the stillness.

"We venerate the lost phallus of our god Osiris. Do him homage!" At these words the multitude fell upon one another in attempt to prostrate before the obelisk. Potiphera began the chant, which was taken up and reverberated by lesser priests.

Manasseh began to cry, and Asenath reached for him in her prone position, pulling him from her back to her breast, where he quieted. It seemed interminable until the loud blast of a trumpet, and everyone stood once again to his feet.

All eyes were riveted upon the tall doors of the temple. The music began again, and bodies began to sway to the rhythm. The doors opened slowly and a minor image of Ra, dressed in a panther skin cape, was carried from the Temple on a palanquin by eight priests of Ra.

Potiphera had silently slipped away from the obelisk, and now he emerged from the Temple wearing his triangular apron and carrying a staff and scepter. He took his place before the image and led the procession to the obelisk. There his family and those of the lesser priests joined him.

Potiphera led the parade across the courtyard of the Temple, through the stone paved streets of the city, to the bank of the Nile River. The multitude sang and danced along the way, tossing streamers and confetti into the morning light. At the river's edge the high priest and his family entered a reed boat with the eight bearers of the image, and began the excursion upriver to the temple at Userkaf, known as the enclosure of the Sun god Ra. The throng followed in a myriad of reed boats.

A special parapet had been erected for Ra in Userkaf before the temple, and there Ra was positioned. Great offerings were made before the idol, keeping the priests busy in carting away the food and flowers, drink offerings and dry goods. Tables were spread with foods of all description. At festival the priests and their families abandoned their dietary dictates and gorged themselves upon vegetables and partook of the various wines. But even festival would not bring a priest or his family to eat the flesh of fish. That was too near to their hearts.

Asenath lost her parents in the crush, but she didn't care. With Manasseh positioned once again on her back, she revelled in the deep red wine in her goblet, savoring the sweet rancid liquid and the flush of excitement that tingled through her veins. She really enjoyed wine, but she was faithful to the gods, and partook of it only at festival. However, when a servant walked about bearing a jug of pungent beer, she extended her goblet for the familiar brew. She ate onions and garlics and leeks in great abundance, until her stomach ached. Finding a spot behind a pillar she emptied her stomach so that she might fill it again.

As the music gained in pitch and volume, the tempo quickened. Worshippers swayed in time with the beat, their bodies careening with obscene gestures and vulgar gyrations. Women danced in wanton abandon, tearing their clothing from their bodies and swaying in erotic movements toward the nearby men. Men plucked their kilts from their bodies, joining the women in licentious dance before the idol.[15] The music blared on, and the singing and laughter rose to a fever pitch. Asenath found herself caught up in the sensual spirit, and slipping from her dress she joined the lewd activities. She removed the band

---

[15] Exodus 32:19,25

which bound Manasseh to her and held the naked infant in her arms, ignoring his loud protests at the sudden jarring movements.

Asenath danced and swayed with complete abandon, her body brushing against those of the naked men and women about her. She laughed and sang loudly, the wine and beer running hot in her veins.

She twirled and fell heavily against someone, and arms clutched her fiercely. Fearing for Manasseh she tried to pull away, and looked up into the austere eyes of her husband. He let go of her and took the wailing infant from her. Then he clutched her arm and pulled her rudely from the horde.

Asenath stopped and pulled back from him. "What are you doing?" she demanded.

"I've come to take you home."

Anger flooded her. Joseph always took things away from her. He didn't want her to have a good time. "You gave me permission to come!"

Joseph tried to pull her along, but she balked. He squinted into her angry eyes. "I didn't know that this would happen."

"What are you talking about?" she shouted at him.

"You are naked!" he shouted back at her. "You are drunk! And you were dancing with naked men." Joseph no longer shouted. He sounded close to tears.

Asenath couldn't understand this man. She sighed and tried to patiently explain. "I only worship my gods. It is part of our religion. You don't understand, Joseph. What we do isn't wrong or bad." She gestured back toward the revelling. "My parents are there. They, too, dance before Ra."

"Naked?"

"Yes."

Joseph was silent, stroking his son's cheek to sooth him, and looking deep into his wife's eyes with his troubled sea green ones. "But you shall not," he said, once again grasping her arm and dragging her along.

Asenath tried to resist, but the wine and beer, coupled with her vigorous dancing, had wearied her, and she was no match for Joseph's strength. She finally submitted and walked with him to a reed boat waiting at the river's edge. There Zedek met them with a cape, which Joseph threw about Asenath's shoulders. She sat sullenly and stared at the river grasses as servants guided the boat to Memphis.

Joseph came to sit at her side, and she turned her face away from him. He spoke softly to her, accompanied by the gentle dip of the oars.

"Please don't be angry. Try to understand that I had to take you away when I learned what happened at festival."

"This is my culture," Asenath answered him in a steely voice. "I am Egyptian."

"No, Asenath, what you were doing is sin," Joseph answered her softly. "You are my wife. I am responsible before God for you. I can't allow it." Joseph took her hand and his voice saddened. "You are my wife. No other man should look upon your nakedness. No other man should..." Joseph's voice broke, and when Asenath turned to him she saw that he wept. "Oh, Asenath," Joseph pleaded through his sorrow, "If only you would turn to the true and living God!"

Asenath was moved by his tears, so she clasped both his hands in hers. "Joseph," she said calmly, "Your God is not my God. I worship the gods of Egypt. That will never change. Just as you will never leave your God for my gods, so I can never leave mine for yours."

Joseph watched her sadly all the way to Memphis.

After that day, Asenath felt the breach grow between them. She and Joseph shared a bed, but little else. He prayed to his God often, in her hearing, begging for her devotion to Him. His eyes were always sad, and he had little to say to her. He spent much time playing with his son, taking him with him to the fields and city, to the desert and river, but without Asenath.

Asenath found herself more and more at the home of

Nophtet, pouring out her woes. Nophtet was a good friend, listening patiently and intently, and offering generous liquid solace. She smiled over Manasseh, but seemed to have no real interest in him. And each time that the two women were together, Nophtet reminded Asenath that love could be found.

"We have a new steward," Nophtet suggested one day as she visited at Asenath's home. She sat scratching Roke's ears and head as the cat purred in her lap. "Next time you come, I'll show him to you. Mmmmmm, he's yummy. I think he could help you drown your sorrows for awhile."

Asenath sat bolt upright at the mention of the steward, reminded of Hoptet and her transgression against Joseph. No, she didn't want a lover. She only wanted Joseph to love her.

When next Joseph and Asenath visited her parents in On, Nofret pulled Asenath aside.

"Natha, whatever happened at the festival of Ra? Suddenly you were missing! We searched for you everywhere until someone told us that your husband had come and taken you away. You said he had given you permission to attend festival."

The burden of Asenath's incompatible life with Joseph was suddenly too much to bear. She struggled with her emotions for a moment, but couldn't hold back the torrent that rushed forth. Collapsing into her mother's arms Asenath wept without words. When at last she could speak she poured out her recent woes.

"It's his God, Mama! Everything that I do to reverence my gods is displeasing to his God. So it's displeasing to Joseph, too!"

Nofret stroked her daughter's long, silky hair. "It has been a great joy to us to have you wed to Egypt's vizier. But his persistence in worshipping the Hebrew God brings us much distress. Your father fears that Apepi is being swayed away from our gods because of Zaphnath's prophecies. It's true that the land gave great yield, but that's a sign only that the gods of Egypt are blessing us greatly. Your father is very cautious about the prophecies of the vizier." She pulled Asenath out at arms length to see into her face. "Be careful, Natha. Don't lose your faith."

"But, Mama, everything I do to venerate our gods is displeasing to Joseph."

"Try to please him in other ways, then, and be discreet about your worship."

When Joseph indicated that it was time to return home, Asenath found Ihat carrying Manasseh in the garden. She reached for the baby, and noticed that Ihat was budding into womanhood. Ihat stroked Manasseh's arm as they walked toward the gate. "He's so beautiful!" she exulted. "His eyes are darker than the vizier's, but he looks very much like him. If Mama will let me, could I come and visit you for awhile? I'd love to spend the time with Manasseh."

Ihat came with a following of servants on the day before Sabbath. Asenath installed her in one of the bedrooms, and then the two spent the day talking. Asenath was amazed how much her sister was growing up, and how well they got along.

On Sabbath, Joseph played games with Asenath and Ihat that he had learned as a child in Canaan. Manasseh toddled along, trying to join in the activity, and Asenath found herself laughing continually at his antics.

When the sun had set and the family sat to eat the evening meal, Ihat nudged close to her and whispered, "You must be very happy married to the vizier. Sabbath is wonderful, even if the servants can't do anything for us. I think the vizier is a lot of fun!"

Asenath considered her sister's words long after they had all gone to their beds. She had never deemed Joseph to be fun. Life was a constant struggle for her against his God. Yet, this day, with her sister here, they had laughed much and she had enjoyed herself.

****

It was Manasseh's first birthday, and Asenath's family would come from On for a celebration. Joseph was at his duties as vizier, and the servants were busy with preparations.

Asenath had abandoned her early morning devotions so that she and Manasseh could pray together to Isis after Joseph left each day. This day she carried Manasseh secretly to the small chapel of Isis. She laid a generous offering of meat and fruits before the idol. Then, taking Manasseh's small hand, she helped him pour out the libation before Isis and her son, Horus. She helped him bow low on his chubby knees before the idol. "Queen of Heaven," she recited, and Manasseh mumbled unintelligible words in mimic. "We praise you... Wife of Osiris...for your blessings." Asenath prayed in phrases as Manasseh clumsily parroted her words.

A rustle sounded behind them, and Asenath instinctively turned. Her heart leapt to her throat as she faced Joseph. He stood with his arms folded across his chest. No expression of his face betrayed the deep anger she heard in his voice.

"Why, Asenath?"

She stood before him, trembling at the fury in his eyes.

"I only pray to my gods."

"You teach Manasseh to bow to your idol!"

Asenath sighed and bit her lip. "Yes," she began softly, but rose in volume as she spoke. "You pray often with Manasseh to your God, and I pray with him to my gods. You teach him about your God and your religion. I teach him about the gods and religion of Egypt. Why not, Joseph? He's my son, too!"

"You teach him to pray to devils!" Joseph shouted. He lifted the tiny chapel and idol above his head and smashed it to the ground, splintering it into a thousand pieces.

CHAPTER 6

"House and riches are the inheritance of fathers: and a prudent wife is from the LORD." Proverbs 19:14

The celebration of Manasseh's first birthday was a strained and uncomfortable event. The tension between Joseph and Asenath crackled through the rooms of the house, touching the guests as well as the honored one. Manasseh sulked and cried, refusing the kisses the family attempted to lavish upon him.

Nikansut chattered excitedly about the priesthood, for which he was making preparations, and Asenath saw Joseph's jaw tighten. "These things you say trouble me," Joseph told him. "To give yourself so devotedly, in such abandon of right and goodness, seems evil to me."

Potiphera cleared his throat loudly and spoke in a deep voice. Asenath knew he was annoyed at Joseph's words. "What we do in the Mysteries cannot be judged by men who have no enlightenment. Right and goodness are irrelevant terms. What we do is right and good because it carries us to a level beyond mortal comprehension."

"But to take a life as part of your rites..." Joseph began.

"The woman is worthless, as chattel. The real purpose for her life is in the losing of it to assist in the elevation of the initiate to the Mysteries."

Joseph shook his head. "All life is given by the Lord God, and the purpose of everyone's life is to know and praise God, to glorify His name." He looked at Nikansut. "I'm sorry to hear that you must do such a brutal deed to please your gods."

Nikansut did not reply. Potiphera quickly asked Joseph a question pertaining to his business as vizier, and Asenath sighed in relief.

When the meal was finished and the servants had carried

around the bowls of water and towels, Asenath and Nofret walked upon the roof garden, arm in arm.

"Well, that conversation was certainly stressful," Nofret said. "But I detect a strain in you, Natha, not caused by today's discussion."

Asenath leaned against her mother's shoulder. "Oh, Mama," she said, the tears coming with a rush of emotion, "Joseph has discovered my little temple and he destroyed it! And Isis, too."

Nofret took Asenath into her arms and cooed to her as to a weeping child, patting and rubbing her back.

Asenath suddenly looked up at her mother through her smeared and streaked makeup. "Mama! Please let Manasseh and me come to your house. Please, Mama, please let us live with you!"

Nofret went rigid and pulled her daughter gently away. "You are the wife of the vizier of Egypt. You will stay here."

"But, Mama."

"No!" Nofret frowned, holding Asenath sternly at arms' length. "You will stay here with your husband!" She released her grip and strode away.

Soon after Asenath's parents went home, she escaped to the pond and dangled her feet. Bright flashes of fish nipped at her toes, but she didn't notice. Her heart was heavy. She was trapped in an impossible marriage, and her own mother had scorned her plea for assistance.

A shadow fell across Asenath's form, and she knew that Joseph sat beside her, but she didn't look at him. He, too, dipped his feet into the pond, sending the fish scattering away.

"Asenath," Joseph said her name softly.

"What." Still she didn't look at him.

"Please forgive my anger this morning."

She didn't answer.

"You do anger me with your stubborn insistence on worshipping your gods, and teaching Manasseh to worship them.

But I'm wrong. You are Egyptian, and you're the daughter of the sun priest." Joseph sighed. "I shouldn't be angry with you. But I want for you to believe in the true God of Heaven and earth. It's very important to me."

Asenath looked at him. She knew this man better than she knew anyone. He sat beside her looking every bit an Egyptian. He was the second ruler in the whole land. But his heart was in contradiction to everything that was Egypt, everything that mattered to her. And her own heart was in contradiction to everything that mattered to him. Two years of marriage to him had not pulled her away from her gods. Neither would another year do so. Joseph knew it. And Asenath knew it.

"Why must it matter so to you?" She asked him softly, touching his gold banded arm. His eyes were sad.

"Because we are one flesh. You are bone of my bones and flesh of my flesh."

"One flesh but two hearts," she said.

"I long for a day when we will have one heart," was his answer.

****

Asenath felt a great need to visit her friend, Nophtet. Leaving Manasseh with his nurse, she was attended by servants to the grand house. Nophtet patiently listened to Asenath's complaints. She was sure that Asenath's goblet was never dry, and she clucked and sighed in sympathy. At last she took Asenath's hand and smiled shrewdly.

"I have a new lover, the most exhilarating yet! He's absolutely gorgeous. Are you ready to consider someone, my friend. I've been saving my steward for you." Nophtet coyly winked at the man as he retrieved a tray of fruits. Asenath kept her eyes away from him.

"If it's love you've found," she asked her friend, "how can

you leave the old lover and find a new one?"

Nophtet laughed. "That's the way it is with love. And there are so many luscious men to love."

Asenath shook her head. "No, Nophtet, I really don't want a lover. I want Joseph to love me."

"Yes, yes, my dear, you do. But he's never going to, is he? He's too wrapped up in that God of his to love his own wife. Think of yourself, Asenath. You deserve to be loved. You deserve to be happy."

"I don't think having an amorous affair would make me happy."

"Then you'll have to resign yourself to misery. The vizier will not love you unless you give up your gods and embrace his. Do you want to be loveless your whole life? You're young, dear friend. You have so much love to give."

"I love Joseph," Asenath said, startling herself at the words.

Nophtet sighed. "What a hopeless mess you're in."

"Yes, it's hopeless."

Asenath went home wondering at her confession. She loved Joseph. Yes, she had known it for quite some time, now, but had just never put it into words. She loved Joseph. And he could never love her!

The inundation of the Nile River had come once more. An invitation came for Joseph to accompany Potiphera and his son, Nikansut on a hippopotamus hunt. The men rode in narrow reed boats poled by servants along the extended edge of the river. There the hippopotami grazed the river bottom. With much excitement and shouting, the men would attempt to spear the large beasts with harpoons.

Asenath sat with her mother beneath a canopy which had been erected along the Nile's surging waters. Servants attended their every whim as they watched Manasseh playing with Ipi and Wehemki. Ihat strolled the riverbank, never getting very far away.

Asenath refreshed herself through the hours with the cool, pungent beer. She and her mother chatted gaily, carefully steering clear of Joseph's God.

At last the women saw the boat coming. The men had finished their hunt. Asenath saw Joseph laughing with her father and brother. She stood and found walking difficult, so she sank back into her seat.

Suddenly Ihat screamed. Her shrieks brought the two women and the servants to the riverbank. Ihat stood helplessly pointing at the water, where three little forms floated among the reeds of the river's edge. Ipi and Wehemki played in the deep waters, laughing and splashing each other. But Manasseh floated helplessly with the current.

The reed boat arrived to the screaming, and Joseph was instantly in the river, pulling his little son from the water. Everyone followed him to the bank, where he sat in the sand and rocked Manasseh back and forth gently. Asenath's heart lurched. She hurried to his side and clutched at Manasseh, who started crying and reached for her.

Joseph stood and surveyed the assembly. Asenath watched him, knowing that he fought hard for control. His voice trembled and threatened collapse as he spoke.

"While you made yourselves drunk, my son almost drowned in the river," he said to his wife and mother in law. To Nofret he said, "This is why I don't approve of Asenath drinking beer."

"She only gets drunk from beer because she's not accustomed to it anymore." Nofret retorted. "There's no harm in beer."

Joseph stared at her soberly. "There was harm today," he said. "We're going home, now, Asenath."

Asenath continued to nurse Manasseh for three years. He would run and play in the grass. He often played with the penned animals, squealing with delight at their antics. Joseph sometimes dove into the pond with his son, letting the little boy splash and kick in the cool water. Then he would run to Mama to breastfeed.

Asenath felt farther from her husband than ever. They shared the common interest of Manasseh, but little else. Asenath avoided his gaze whenever possible, and Joseph seemed to avoid time alone with her, for neither one knew what to talk about. The matter dearest to their hearts could not be discussed.

Without being asked, Nofret sent another, smaller image of Isis and Horus, as well as masons to build another small chapel. Asenath found a spot behind the animal pens, shielded by tall grasses, for the chapel. She and Manasseh resumed their daily devotions with offerings to their gods.

Manasseh had stumbled with words for several weeks, but once he grasped language his vocabulary grew quickly, and he could talk fluently even with adults.

Egypt was nearing the harvest of the third year of Joseph's guidance as vizier, and more barns had been built to accommodate all the increase. Joseph and Asenath, with Manasseh and several servants in tow, had gone to the river's edge for a Sabbath picnic. The servants spread the meal on blankets beneath the scant shade afforded by date palms along the water's edge. Remembering Manasseh's dowsing in the river, Asenath kept him close and watched him carefully. Joseph stood at the riverbank and Asenath sat in the shade. Each watched the river, deep in private thoughts. Suddenly Manasseh grasped his father's hand and pulled Joseph over to where Asenath sat, and Joseph sat beside her. Manasseh's cherub face smiled at his father.

"Papa," he chirped, "Mama and I love our gods. I give cakes to the Queen of Heaven. Mama wishes we had beer instead of just nectar to offer."

A deathly silence followed the little boy's cheerful words. Joseph didn't look at Manasseh or his wife. He stared out over the silvery waters of the Nile. Asenath saw his shoulders shudder. Joseph had no answer for his son, so, making no reply he stood to his feet. He looked quickly at Asenath and then walked away from the river. Asenath assigned the nurse to look after Manasseh and then scrambled after Joseph.

He walked along wordlessly, Asenath hurrying to keep up. When they had put a distance between themselves and the servants, Joseph stopped and turned to her.

"You still teach my son to pray to your gods against my will," he said accusingly.

"You ask too much," she defended herself. "What you ask of me isn't fair."

"I can't stop you, apparently, from worshipping your idols. But I don't want Manasseh worshipping them."

"You can't stop me from teaching him," she answered defiantly. "I am his mother. You teach him about your God and I teach him about mine." Asenath looked boldly into Joseph's sad aqua eyes. "What makes your God better than mine? What harm is there for Manasseh to learn both our religions?"

Joseph sighed deeply. "I wish with all my heart that you could understand the difference. The God I love and reverence is the Almighty Creator of Heaven and earth. He is the source and sustainer of all life." He swallowed and looked intently at his wife. "He is the one, true, and only God, Asenath. The gods of Egypt are the product of man's minds and hands. If there is any power behind them at all it's only the evil power of God's enemy, Satan." Joseph watched the muscle of Asenath's jaw twitch, and he continued. "It matters what Manasseh believes. He must not give reverence to idols of wood or stone. He must love and trust the true God of Heaven and earth."

Asenath squinted at the powerful man before her and asked in disdain, "You live in the land of Egypt and yet you defy her gods? Would you defy the gods of your pharaoh, Apepi?" She trembled with the disgrace of it.

"No, Asenath," Joseph answered her calmly. "I don't defy Egypt's gods. I only say that they are idols of stone that can't see or hear or answer prayer. The true God of Heaven and earth alone has power to answer prayer, and He alone should be worshipped."

"I prayed to Isis for a son," Asenath reminded him. "Has your God answered your prayers? He allowed you to be sold as a slave and then wrongfully accused. You lived in prison for years. Has He allowed you to return to your father? No! Your God doesn't answer prayer. How dare you mock my gods?"

Joseph fell on his knees and closed his eyes. Somewhat startled, Asenath knelt beside him. Joseph spoke, but not to her.

"Holy God, I love You and praise Your name. Thank You for keeping me through my years of servitude and imprisonment. Thank You for delivering me from prison. Thank You for giving me a beautiful and good wife." A sob escaped him, but he continued to pray. "She doesn't know You, Lord. She is devout and faithful to the gods of Egypt, but she doesn't know You." He paused. "Thank You for our son, Manasseh. My desire for him, O God, is that he will learn to love and trust you. I want him to be a man of God." Another sob. "Asenath doesn't understand this, Lord. She can't see the importance of Manasseh trusting only You. Will You work in her heart, Lord God? I can't. I've tried, but Lord You know I can't make her understand. And, Lord, I'm concerned for Asenath. With all her devotion to her gods, she's lost. Show Yourself to her, God. Let her come to trust in You. She says she will never turn from her gods to You, but You have all power." Joseph paused again and sighed deeply. "What Asenath said is true, Lord. I have prayed through these years that I may see my father again. Keep my faith in You, and don't let me waver, my God. I don't understand, but help me know I don't need to understand. Let me trust in You, alone."

Both were silent. Joseph remained on his knees with closed eyes. Asenath remained at his side. He had not spoken to her, but he had allowed her to hear the deepest desires of his heart. He had called her "lost." She wanted an explanation, but couldn't ask him. She looked at him and her heart lurched. He had pulled his heavy woolen wig from his head and his wavy hair reflected the desert sand. He was a stranger in her land, the vizier of Egypt. She was moved to put her arms around him, but didn't. She sat quietly, waiting.

Joseph finally raised his eyes to hers. They swam with tears which dripped along his nose. "Will you promise me not to take Manasseh to your idol?" he asked quietly.

"Why should I?" she began, but his beautiful eyes imploring sadly altered her reply. "Yes."

"You will promise?"

"Yes."

Joseph sighed and straightened his back. "Would you get rid of your idol?" His eyes were hopeful.

"If I did I would still venerate Isis in my heart. I've promised not to take our son to Isis. But I can't promise the same for me. Please, Joseph, don't ask it."

Joseph stood and pulled Asenath to her feet. "This is really hard for both of us, isn't it?" he asked kindly. "Our lives are in constant conflict. I wish it wasn't that way. I had always thought that a man and his wife should be best friends, not enemies. Sometimes I feel that's what we are, Asenath, warring with each other because I trust in God and you in idols."

Tears coursed down Asenath's face and Joseph brushed them from her cheek with his thumb. Then, embracing her, Joseph kissed her tenderly. She only cried the more. Joseph smiled wanly at her.

"My dearest desire is that you will trust the Lord God of Heaven. I know I can't force you to. But I don't want to war with you. How can we have peace?"

Asenath sniffed. "I will try. For Manasseh's sake." She paused. Should she tell him, now? Yes, she should tell him while his arms were around her, and his heart was gentle toward her. "And for the child who grows beneath my heart."

Joseph pulled her out to arms' length and hope and regret battled in his eyes. "Are you with child?" he asked.

Asenath bit her lip. "Yes."

Joseph watched her silently for a moment. "We will not quarrel over this child." His statement held a question.

"I promise I will not teach this child the ways of Egypt's gods," she whispered.

Joseph smiled. "Thank you," he said, and drew her close again.

CHAPTER 7

"The curse of the LORD is in the house of the wicked, but he blesseth the habitation of the just." Proverbs 3:33

Asenath resumed her early morning vigil to the tiny chapel of Isis, accompanied only by Roke. There she offered small cakes, and there she poured out the nectar of fruits before her gods. She paused in her devotions to fight the nausea which rose in her stomach. When the wave had passed she knelt low before the stone image of Isis and Horus.

"Oh Queen of Heaven, wife of Osiris, I beg of you to make this child a daughter. I want no more sons to be mutilated by the barbaric ritual of circumcision. Please let this child be a girl."

This prayer had become her morning liturgy. So sure was she that Isis had given her a son the first time, that she made this request with confidence.

"You must understand, Oh wife of Osiris, Zaphnathpaaneah has forbidden me to bring Manasseh before you. It was not my choice. I have told you the things the Pharaoh's vizier requires of me. Please don't let his decision close your ears to my request for a daughter."

Asenath sat back on her heels, remembering Joseph's words to her father, "He has eyes," Joseph had observed, "but does he see you? He has ears, but does he hear?"

Fear suddenly tore her thoughts away from Joseph's words. She dared not doubt her gods.

Asenath had kept her word to Joseph. Manasseh soon forgot his prayers to Isis, and now began to speak of Joseph's God, sometimes even in Hebrew, the language of Joseph's people.

"Yadah Yehovah," he would say as he played about the house.

"What are you saying, Manasseh?" Asenath asked.

"I am praising the name of my God," the child answered.

"And who is your God?" she asked.

"My God is the Creator of Heaven and earth."

"What is your God's name?"

Manasseh paused in his play, "His name is Jehovah. He is the Lord, God."

"What does he look like?"

The child studied her question. "Papa says that God is a spirit, and that man was made in his image. Perhaps God looks like a man."

"Have you ever seen Him, Manasseh?"

"No, Mama. Papa hasn't seen Him, either. But we know that He hears our prayers."

"How do you know?"

"Because we love Him and trust Him."

Asenath sighed, somewhat guilty at drilling her small son. Joseph had forbidden her to teach him about her gods, and she would keep her promise, but perhaps her questions would raise doubts in the boy's mind, and he would ask to learn of her gods on his own.

The overflowing of the Nile along its shoreline extended farther than had ever been recorded. The flood waters endured longer than usual, abating only just in time for the planters to wade about in the muddy fields and sow the grain. The crops which sprang up in the deep, rich deposits of the inundation were strong and healthy, yielding a great increase. So much had been stored by this fourth year of plenty that the scribes had left off recording, and Joseph had quit counting. He only knew that His God had caused the crops to grow in great abundance, leaving much extra beyond the needs of the Egyptian people.

Asenath wondered how it happened that Joseph's God could make such a thing occur in Egypt. What of Egypt's gods? Why would they sit idly by and let a foreign God receive the honor for the blessings of the harvest? Her mind reeled in confusion, but she faithfully prayed to Isis.

Nophtet sighed and shook her head at Asenath's pregnancy. "I fear babies will keep you from ever finding love."

Asenath didn't find her visits with her friend as satisfying as in the past days. Nophtet's only interest seemed to be finding a paramour for her. She stayed as long as necessary, and then returned home.

"Mama!" Manasseh cried, running to her, his short kilt slapping his legs, his tears smeared with blood on his face. "Roke scratched me!"

Asenath knelt and wiped his face with the edge of her linen gown. "What did you do to her?" she asked gently.

Manasseh stuck out his lower lip and frowned.

"Did you pull her tail?"

Manasseh nodded his head, his lip still stuck out.

Asenath gathered her son into her arms, stifling a laugh. "You must be kind to Roke if you want her to be kind to you." She paused. "Soon you'll have a little sister. You will need to always be kind to her."

"Did God tell you that our baby will be a sister?" he asked.

"I have prayed and asked Isis to give you a sister."

Manasseh furrowed his brow. "Papa told me that only the Lord God can answer prayers. He told me that the gods that you and Pippa serve are only idols of stone who can't answer prayers."

Asenath suddenly grew hot. She dismissed her child to play and began to pace the room in agitation. Joseph had gone too far, now. She folded her arms above her swollen belly and paced in the awkward gait of full pregnancy. She scowled at Zedek when he entered the room, and he hurried away, keeping a safe distance from her.

When Joseph returned home that evening she met him at the door. Her arms were folded across her chest, and she still scowled. Joseph stopped before her, dismayed at her visage and demeanor. He waited for her to speak.

Asenath had determined to speak in a controlled manner, but when she opened her mouth her voice was high pitched. "Why do you poison our son against the gods of Egypt?"

Totally unprepared for the outburst which met him, Joseph frowned, digesting her words. He closed the door behind him and taking her arm led her to a seat. He sat at her side, holding her hand although she tried to pull it away. "What are you talking about?" he asked.

"You teach Manasseh that the gods of Egypt cannot answer prayer," she said shrilly. "I do not teach him to pray to Isis, but I don't speak against your God!" Her conscience pricked her slightly with memory, but she pushed that thought away. Joseph was openly teaching Manasseh against the gods of Egypt.

Joseph nodded, comprehension dawning. "Yes, I have taught Manasseh that only Jehovah God can answer prayer." Asenath jerked her hand from him and stood up, pointing an accusing finger at him.

"You admit it, then!" she screamed.

"But only God can answer prayer, Asenath," Joseph said, standing, too. "I know that you pray to Isis, but I must teach Manasseh the truth."

"Truth according to you!" Asenath screamed at him.

"It is the truth," Joseph said softly.

Asenath collapsed in tears upon a chair. "This is so unfair," she cried. "You live in Egypt! Manasseh is my son, too! Why must you teach him against my gods?"

"I must only teach my son the truth, Asenath."

The man was impossible! Asenath fled to the bedroom and fell upon the bed in frustrated tears.

She heard him enter with a servant, but kept her face to the wall.

"I had our supper brought here," he said. She remained silent and motionless.

Joseph approached and sat on the bed at her side. He touched her arm gently. "Asenath," he said. She did not answer. "I don't want you to hate me. We're so different, and you can't understand about worship of Jehovah. But please don't hate me."

Asenath had not imagined Joseph would ever say such a thing. She rolled over slowly until she could see him. "I don't hate you," she said softly. She reached out and touched his golden hair.

Joseph pulled her hand to his lips. Asenath's heart cried out, "Please love me, Joseph, even though I don't pray to your God," but her voice did not.

Asenath was sorting through her baby linens when Zedek announced Nophtet. Her friend entered the room regally as usual, but her eyes were red and swollen beneath the thick kohl. Asenath dismissed the servants who came bearing water to wash her guest's feet. Nophtet sat rigidly, her haughty expression in place, but the knuckles of her tightly clasped hands white.

Asenath sat waiting for her friend to speak. Nophtet's gray eyes started to tear, but she said composedly, "I am with child."

Asenath smiled, taking her hand. "It's not that bad," she said, patting her own belly. "You'll get your figure back soon after, and babies are such a joy! And the Venerable Jash will be proud."

"No," Nophtet said sternly, "I will not have this child."

"Please don't say that," Asenath pleaded softly. "You'll love your baby, as I do mine, even this one," she said, patting her belly again.

Nophtet stood suddenly and began to pace. "But your babies are the vizier's children. This child does not belong to the Venerable Jash."

Asenath sat silently. The severity of the situation began to dawn. If the Venerable Jash knew this could not be his child, then surely his wife's indiscretions would be discovered. An indiscreet wife could be flogged to death, or sold into slavery.

"I have found a woman who takes care of these things," Nophtet said. "But her price is high." She turned to face Asenath. "You are the only one I know to turn to. Can you get some money for me? I can't use Jash's money, or he'll find out! Please help me!"

Nophtet's frigid facade broke into weeping, and Asenath stood and embraced her friend. She had no money of her own. Zedek saw to all purchases for the household. Joseph had always given her money when she asked, but how could she ask him for this? She knew he would deny her this.   "How much do you need?"

"A thousand ontoons."

"So much?"

"For such a great service as this woman can offer, no price is too much. But I can't get the money from Jash!"

"Let me think," Asenath told her, pacing the room herself. It was impossible to get it without Joseph knowing. Zedek would certainly tell Joseph if she ordered a thousand ontoons. But what about her father? He had money like that, and Joseph would never know if she got it from her father. But what could she tell him? He would surely want to know its purpose, and she couldn't tell him the truth, for he was a long acquaintance of the Venerable Jash. She would ask Isis for aid, and then she would think of something.

"I will get it for you."

"How soon?"

"Perhaps tomorrow, or a few days, but I'll have it delivered as soon as I have it."

Nophtet regained her composure and held a hand out to Asenath. "Thank you, friend."

Asenath had tried to sound casual as she announced her desire to visit her mother the next day. Joseph frowned, looking at her distended belly. "I don't think it's wise," he told her. "You're too close to delivery."

Her mind whirled, seeking a solution, and she wished she had not asked. She would go anyway, even if he refused her request, and face the consequences later. Nophtet needed her help.

Early the next morning Asenath prostrated herself as well as possible before her gods. "Oh, Queen of Heaven! My friend has been indiscreet and is with child with a man other than her husband." Asenath dared not mention Nophtet's name, lest somehow Isis should reveal the dark deed to the Venerable Jash. "I have promised to get gold for her to take care of the problem. Widow of Osiris, I know that Zaphnathpaaneah will not give me the sum my friend needs. I beg your aid as I petition my father, Potiphera, Priest of On, for the gold. Please intercede to the great sun god, Ra, on my behalf, and let my father give me the gold."

When Joseph had gone, Asenath quickly ordered a boat to On. Leaving Manasseh in the care of his nurse and accompanied by her maids and several strong oarsmen, she made the trip to On. How silly of Joseph to deny me, she thought. I still have a fortnight to go, and a visit to my parents is good for me, isn't it? She pushed aside the guilt that gnawed at her disobedience to Joseph, and set her mind on the task ahead.

Potiphera was at the Temple of Ra, and when he saw Asenath beckoning him from the main entrance, he left his duties to another and greeted her.

"Natha, I'm surprised to see you so close to the birthing of your child. Is Zaphnath with you?"

"No, Papa, I came alone."

Potiphera raised an eyebrow and guided his daughter into an adjoining room. "What is it?" he asked.

"Papa, I need a thousand ontoons."

His eyes widened at the sum. "Hasn't your husband money to meet your needs and wants?"

"He does, Papa, but I can't tell him about this. I can't tell you what it's for, either, but it means a lot to me. I couldn't ask him for the money, because he would insist on knowing the purpose." She looked beseechingly into her father's eyes. "Please don't ask me what it's for, Papa. I can't tell you. But I need a thousand ontoons."

Potiphera had seldom denied his children a request. Yet, he hesitated at the great amount of gold that she asked. Finally he called a lesser priest to him.

"Call my steward here," he commanded.

Potiphera and Asenath waited in the Temple garden for the steward. Goblets of beer were brought, and Asenath relaxed beneath the shade of the flowering trees, imbibing the dark liquid. Now, with beer in her blood, she finally felt calm. Her father would give her the money, and she had no need to fear.

When the steward came, Asenath heard her father order the gold from his coffers. She continued to calm her nerves with beer until the steward returned with a small, but heavy chest.

"Take it," Potiphera told her, gesturing toward the chest, which a servant would bear home for her. "I wish to never know the reason."

Asenath hugged her father and kissed his smooth cheek, thanking him profoundly, and then departed for Memphis.

Upon reaching the quay, Asenath ordered the chest to be borne to the home of the Venerable Jash, and delivered only into the hands of that great man's wife. Then, confident in her deception, she stopped at the Temple of Apis to leave a thank offering before returning to her home.

And there he stood, waiting for her. Joseph's arms were across his chest, and his eyes sparked fire. But Asenath saw a sadness in his handsome face. She swallowed and took a deep breath before she faced him.

"Did you go to On?" he asked.

"Yes."

"Why did you go when I told you not to?"

"I wanted very much to see my father."

Joseph's severe gaze was too much for her, so she looked

away and tried to walk away. But he reached suddenly and grasped both her arms. The anger was gone when she looked up into his face, and only the sadness remained.

"My men intercepted a servant bearing a chest of gold, which he said that you had ordered to the wife of the Venerable Jash. Why did you get a thousand ontoons from Potiphera and send them to the wife of the Venerable Jash?"

How did he know? How could he have found her out? As she looked into his sad blue green eyes, she was instantly sorry that she had tried to deceive him. But it had been done. What could she say?

Joseph waited. Finally Asenath knew that she must tell him. He would detect an untruth, she was certain.

"My friend needs the gold to rid herself of an unwanted pregnancy."

His eyes narrowed, and he furrowed his brow. "You would help her do such a thing?"

"You don't understand," she said.

"Explain it to me."

What could she say? Would Joseph take the awful truth to the Venerable Jash, and destroy Nophtet's life? She didn't know, but she knew that she must tell him.

"The child does not belong to the Venerable Jash."

Joseph's voice was choked as he asked, "Why would you help her kill an innocent child for such a reason?" He laid a hand on her abdomen, where her unborn baby slept.

Asenath looked into her husband's beautiful eyes and realized that he did not understand the ways of Egypt. "She and the innocent child will die if the Venerable Jash so chooses."

Joseph nodded. "But you will not help her. I will send the gold back to Potiphera."

When Joseph had returned to his duties as vizier of Egypt, Asenath composed a note to her friend. "I had the gold, but my husband discovered it, and has returned it to my father. Please forgive my failure." she wrote. Summoning a servant, she sent the epistle to Nophtet, then went to her bedroom and wept. The first twinge of labor awakened Asenath while it was yet dark. According to her calculations, this should not happen yet, but she knew a baby would come when it would come. She was determined not to call the midwife hours before she was needed as last time. Asenath paced the dark rooms breathing as the midwife had taught her at Manasseh's birth. She wanted to pray to Isis, but didn't dare descend to her tiny chapel in the dark night and in labor. Besides, the failure of Isis to help her with the gold for Nophtet nagged at her mind. She thought of Joseph's God, to Whom he prayed anywhere, anytime. A pang of labor compressed her and she thought about calling out to Joseph's God for help. Suddenly angry at herself for such thoughts she began to march about in irritation. She was weary from sleeplessness and pacing the floors, but she couldn't sit or lie down in comfort. Perspiration flowed down her face and neck. She found the breathing inadequate to help her through the pains and finally cried out.

Joseph was instantly at her side, holding her as she was seized with pain.

"How long?" he asked.

Unsure whether he meant the time elapsed or the time to go, she shook off his arms as her contraction passed and resumed walking.

"Should I call the midwife?" Joseph asked, pacing beside her.

"Not yet," she said.

"Would you like something to eat or drink?" Joseph asked.

"No!" she snapped, another contraction seizing her. Joseph stood by helplessly as she suffered alone. When she began to pace again she took a step and collapsed on the floor. Joseph gathered her into his arms while shouting for his steward.

Zedek stumbled up the stairs from the servants' quarters carrying a small clay lamp. As soon as he entered the room

Joseph sent him for the midwife.

Joseph laid Asenath on the bed and ordered a servant, who had come up at the noise, to bring water and a cloth. He bathed her brow and spoke soothingly as she groaned. As another contraction came upon her she clutched Joseph's arm.

"The baby's coming!" she screamed.

Joseph positioned himself to help her.

"I need the birthing stool!" she shrieked as her second son was born, without a birthing stool.

When the midwife arrived she found an exhausted mother, a fatigued father, and a peacefully sleeping infant.

Joseph knelt at the bedside, gently stroking the tiny hand. Asenath touched the hands of father and son tenderly, the terrors of childbirth past and forgotten. She looked at the golden glow of Joseph's head, bowed over her child, and her heart swelled with love for the man who had helped her bring her child into the world.

"I will call him Ephraim," Joseph said softly, "for God has caused me to be fruitful in the land of my affliction."[16]

Asenath kissed the top of Ephraim's head. "I prayed to Isis for a daughter," she said.

Joseph continued to stroke the baby's hand. "Why a daughter?" he asked.

"I hate your rite of circumcision."

Joseph was quiet, stroking the hand.

"Isis didn't give me a daughter," Asenath said quietly.

Joseph looked at her, his beautiful eyes weary and sad. "Only Jehovah, the Lord God, gives life." He looked at his son. "Children are a gift from God. He alone has given us this son."

Asenath sighed and kissed her baby again. This child, fruit of her body as well as his, had been promised to Joseph's God.

---

[16] Genesis 41:52

On the eighth day, Joseph brought Manasseh to his knee as he circumcised Ephraim. When the crying infant had been handed to his mother for comfort, Joseph took Manasseh on his lap and talked to him about Abraham, Isaac, and Jacob, the child's own ancestors. He taught Manasseh the commandment of the Lord, and how circumcision set him apart as one of the chosen ones of the Lord God.

Potiphera and his family came to see the new son of the vizier. Ipi and Wehemki, attending school now and wearing knee length kilts, sat about more calmly, sharing their experiences from school. They recited lessons to Asenath until Nofret sent them outside to play with Manasseh. Ihat sat silently, aware that the vizier's eyes never rested on her. She now wore her hair long and crimped and dressed in the manner of young women. Asenath had tried to explain Joseph's strange ways to her mother and sister, but they couldn't fully grasp it.

Nikansut couldn't stay still. He fidgeted until he had opportunity to speak.

"I'll go to the Temple Pyramid, soon, to be initiated into the Mysteries," he told Asenath excitedly.

She smiled at him. "I'm happy for you, Niki."

"After I'm initiated, I shall take a wife."

"Niki! Who is she?"

"Ismala, the daughter of Sahure, of the Temple of Ra."

"I know her!" Asenath exulted. "She and I played together as children. I'm so happy for you, Niki!"

When the meal was served and the children came into the house, Manasseh stood near his grandfather, leaning on his knee. He looked up into Potiphera's face intently. "Mama prayed to Isis for a sister, but the Lord God gave us a brother instead."

Asenath blushed and warmed with embarrassment. Potiphera lifted the child onto his knee and said, "Isis does not always give sisters or brothers when asked."

The child answered confidently, "Isis is only an image of stone, Pippa. It is the Lord God alone Who can answer prayer.

Jehovah is the giver of life. He is the one Who gave us our Ephraim."

Silence fell on the room.

"If you've finished your meal, Manasseh, run outdoors and play," Asenath suggested.

When the children had departed, Potiphera cleared his throat. His son in law was his superior in the kingdom of Egypt, but as the priest of the sun god, Ra, he felt impelled to speak to him about Manasseh's declaration.

"Do you teach my grandson these things?" Potiphera asked Joseph.

"I must teach my son the truth."

"You live in the land of Egypt, which is guarded by the gods of Egypt, and yet you teach the grandson of the priest of Ra that our gods are only images of stone, unable to answer prayer?"

"I must teach my son the truth."

Potiphera visibly repressed his emotions, touching his fingertips together beneath his chin and breathing deeply. When he spoke his voice was composed.

"You have lived in Egypt many years, now, Zaphnathpaaneah, and have served well as the vizier of our land," he said, reverting to the original designation given by Pharaoh. "In all this time have you not seen the merit of venerating our gods?"

"I trust Jehovah, the Creator of Heaven and earth. He alone is God, and it is He alone that I worship."

Potiphera held his posture, but frowned deeply.

"Papa," Asenath said softly. "I have long wondered, now, why the gods of Egypt permit Joseph's God to receive the recognition for making the crops of Egypt grow in great plenty."

Potiphera's face relaxed and he nodded slowly. "The gods of Egypt are they that control the waters of the Nile, the wind, the sun, and the growth of crops." He paused and turned his gaze to Joseph. "The God of Zaphnathpaaneah has received credit for the great abundance of Egypt's harvest only because our great Apepi believes that his dream was interpreted with accuracy by the vizier."

Asenath waited for Joseph to reply to the insinuation made by her father, but he was silent, and his expression remained the same.

Potiphera continued. "As the priest of the god Ra I must believe that the blessings come from my gods. I wonder at the opinion of the Pharaoh, for he is the very incarnation of Horus on earth. Although I will not oppose my king, my faith remains strong in the gods of Egypt."

"I must respect your position, Father in law," Joseph said, nodding his head toward Potiphera. "But it is the prayer of my heart to the Lord God that you and all of yours will someday come to trust Him alone."

Asenath looked at her husband amazed. She knew that was his constant prayer for her, but she had not realized that he prayed for her family as well, to believe in his God.

"There remain yet two years of plenty," Joseph told his father in law. "When the Lord God cuts off the waters of the Nile and the land of Egypt knows famine perhaps then you will believe in Him."

Potiphera was silent, considering Joseph's words. Then he shook his head. "The gods of Egypt have blessed the land better some years than others, but never has the land known famine." He looked his son in law squarely in the eyes. "If indeed such famine as you speak of comes to Egypt, for seven years as you say, I will be compelled to consider the merits of your God. But that remains to be seen." He folded his arms across his chest and smiled smugly.

Asenath put off a visit to Nophtet until she could bear it no longer. She knew that it would have been public knowledge had the Venerable Jash chastised his wife with whipping or slavery, and she had heard nothing. Perhaps he did not yet know of the child growing in his wife's womb. But he soon would. It could not be hidden forever. She must see her friend and learn what she planned to do.

Asenath was ushered into Nophtet's grand home, and found her friend seated on a plush couch. Nophtet rose and greeted her cheerily, as always before, and ordered a foot washing and beer.

When the servants had finished and gone, Asenath said, "Did you get my note? I'm sorry about the gold."

Nophtet smiled, waving her hand as if to dismiss the apology. "You did your best, I can ask no more. But the gods took care of me. The child died by natural causes."

"A miscarriage?"

"Yes. And I have vowed to double my offerings to the gods. I can't understand, though, why the Vizier of Egypt did not share the dark knowledge with the Venerable Jash."

Asenath saw accusation in her friend's eyes. "I had to tell Joseph the truth," she tried to explain. "I find that I can't lie to him. And I don't know why he didn't tell your husband."

Nophtet smiled again. "It seems that the gods of Egypt can govern even the actions of the vizier."

Asenath shook her head. "No, I don't think it was Egypt's gods that kept him from it. I don't believe the gods of Egypt have the least bit of power in Joseph's life. His God is his life."

Nikansut began his initiation into the Mysteries with a grand banquet given by Apepi at the palace at Memphis, which Joseph and Asenath attended. The Pharaoh presented a written authorization to the priests of On, to Potiphera in particular as the high priest. Following the banquet, Nikansut was referred to the learned men of the Institution of the Mysteries at Memphis, who, after instructing him, escorted him to Giza, to the Great Pyramid.

Asenath and Joseph accompanied her family as they followed Nikansut to the Great Pyramid. There they watched as two Thesmophores, or indroductors, climbed with Nikansut up the smooth casing stones of the pyramid about fifty feet, attended by a dozen slaves. The slaves, at the direction of the Thesmophores, grasped the stone door, which was indistinguishable from the other casing stones, and swung it on its swivel hinge. When Nikansut and the Thesmophores had entered the pyramid temple, the stone was replaced, leaving the stone face smooth and undisturbed. If successful in his apprenticeship, Nikansut would remain within the confines of the Great Pyramid for a full year.

Two children made the acquiring of another nurse necessary. Asenath's life was full of managing her household, overseeing the care of her two sons, and fulfilling her obligations to the court of Pharaoh. However, at such occasions of state, she began to grow uneasy as she drank her favorite beverage, Egypt's strong grain beer, beneath the gaze of her husband. Even at her parent's house, she began to cringe as Joseph looked on at her drinking of beer. Only at Nophtet's home, where she visited without Joseph, could she truly enjoy the beer.

One day, as she relaxed with a goblet of beer at Nophtet's home, she was startled at her friend's declaration. "Since you didn't want my steward, I have decided to have him myself. He is a little shy, and inexperienced, but I must tell you that you gave up something quite remarkable."

In Asenath's mind she saw a young Hebrew steward with a mistress quite like her friend, pursuing him, and imploring him to be her lover. Asenath suddenly pitied the steward of Nophtet, and was thankful for the strength that the Hebrew steward had had against the temptation.

"Why do you still pursue indiscretions after what happened?" she asked.

Nophtet's eyes narrowed, and she leaned toward Asenath. "I cannot live without love. Even though your husband doesn't return your love, still, as you say, you love him. I could never love Jash. He's old, and ugly, and smelly. At least the vizier is extremely handsome. I must be loved."

Asenath suddenly felt sorry for her friend, too. Nophtet

had never found love with her many paramours. Even to love without being loved in return was better than Nophtet's pursuits.

Every seventh day was Sabbath, and Asenath soon grew accustomed to fending for herself as the servants rested. Indeed she looked forward to the day of rest, for Joseph would spend the entire day at home, playing with his sons, talking with her. She endured the yearly sacrifice of a lamb to Jehovah, watching her small sons listen intently and watch with wide eyes as their father shed the blood of the lamb, and taught them about Messiah. But Asenath's prayers were still recited daily before the small stone image of Isis and her son, Horus.

Asenath saw her family often, asking always about Nikansut's progress. For the first few months he was imprisoned in the Subterranean Chamber of the Great Pyramid, attended by initiates. There he would write his thoughts and spend the time in reflection. He could have no outside contact during this time, even with the Demiurgos, or Chief Inspector of the Society of the Mysteries, who was Potiphera the priest of On.

When Nikansut's duration in the vault was finished, Potiphera gave glowing accounts of his great progress in the grade of Pastophoris, the First Grade. The ordeal of flashing lights and noise of thunder which were artificially induced to terrify the long entombed apprentice had not discouraged him. Nikansut had taken his oaths of fidelity and discretion, learning the secret grip of the hand and the secret word. He was stripped and cleansed and then clothed in a pyramidical shaped hood, the triangular apron, and a collar with long tassels. Until the conclusion of the year, it was his duty to act as Guard of the Subterranean Chamber.

Joseph and Asenath attended a celebration at the home of Potiphera for Nikansut. He had passed the severe test to prepare him for the grade of Neocoris, the Second Grade. As Neocoris, it was his duty to wash the columns of the Grotto of the Initiates, and he could come and go daily to complete his tasks.

Nikansut's eyes glowed with the knowledge he had

acquired while preparing for the Mysteries. He related the trials of the great test.

"When my year was complete I was served a delicious meal by beautiful women. The meal smelled delectable and the women were seductive in every way, but it was my duty to resist both the food and the women. This trial continued for many hours. When at last I had triumphed and had affirmed such to the assembly of initiates, I was doused with water to purify me." He looked at his younger brothers and nephew. "Then a poisonous serpent was thrown over my body, which I had to allow to slither over my body and then collect into my apron."

The boys uttered their esteem for Nikansut, their eyes glowing with admiration.

"Everyone else left the chamber," Nikansut continued, "and it was suddenly filled with crawling reptiles, snakes, and lizards. My duty was to withstand bodily terror. I can't explain to you how terrible it was. But I was greatly lauded at my reception for showing courage. I was given my insignia and the word of my grade, which I cannot share with you."

When they had returned to their home, Manasseh sat on Joseph's lap, fingering his gold necklace. "When I am grown up I want to be an apprentice like Uncle Niki," he said.

Joseph rubbed the little boy's back and closed his eyes. Then he pulled the child's face around to see into his eyes. "Uncle Niki doesn't believe in the Lord God, the Creator of Heaven and earth. He worships the gods of Egypt, and the Mysteries are part of his worship of his gods. You trust in Jehovah, Manasseh, the true and living God. You will never be a part of the Mysteries."

Asenath left the room to nurse her younger son. He, too, would learn these same things from Joseph as he grew. Somehow, hearing him speak such things no longer pained her as deeply as they once had. Perhaps she was getting used to hearing them.

When the boys were both in bed and the servants tended

their evening chores, Joseph took Asenath's hand and led her out the door onto the balcony. They leaned against the edge and looked over the city of Memphis spread before them, glittering in its lamplight in the darkness. The waters of the Nile were a dark ribbon cutting through the shimmering lights. The continual lights surrounding the Temples of Apis and Ptah caused a glow against the sky. Far above, the stars blinked in their cold canopy of space.

"One year of plenty remains," Joseph said. "Then the famine will begin and the people of Egypt will be fed with the stores we have put aside during the plenty." He looked at Asenath in the soft light from the window. "Your father told me that he will reconsider the Lord when the famine comes. Will you consider trusting in Him, Asenath?"

Asenath stared out over the city. "Do you really believe there will be seven years of famine?"

"I do. I know there will be."

She turned and looked at him. "I've always trusted in Isis. To even say that I could trust in your God could bring the wrath of Egypt's gods upon me."

"Egypt's gods have no power before the Lord God. Will you put your trust in Him when He brings the famine?"

Asenath saw pleading in Joseph's beautiful turquoise eyes. She wished that she could see love there, too. She knew that even a promise to trust in his God if famine came would please him. But she did not believe; she could not promise.

"The gods of Egypt have allowed your God to take the praise for the great plenty of the land. But they won't let a famine come. They won't allow your God to receive any more honor." She left his side and went back into the house.

****

"You were sixteen when you married, weren't you?" Ihat asked one day.

"I was," Asenath answered, remembering her fear of the criminal, and then the recognition of his identity.

"I'm sixteen," Ihat said. "And Papa told me that he must soon find a suitable husband for me." She sat heavily on a chair and put her elbows on her knees, cupping her chin in her hands. "I think he is very immersed in Niki's initiation, right now, but when that's completed, he'll start looking for a husband for me."

Asenath sat by her sister, and Ihat was suddenly in her position of old, sitting on the floor with her arms on Asenath's lap.

"What will I do if he's old, and ugly?" she implored.

Asenath thought of Nophtet, who had never accepted her marriage, and could never find happiness. "You will love him and be a good wife to him, no matter what he is like," she told her sister.

"You can say that, because your husband is handsome and kind. But I don't know if Papa will find such a wonderful husband for me. I doubt very much that there's anyone in Egypt like the vizier." She paused, looking into Asenath's face. "I would like to marry a man with blue green eyes like the vizier's. Even if he were old and ugly, blue green eyes would make me happy."

"You're being silly," Asenath laughed. Yes, she loved Joseph's blue green eyes. But there was so much more about Joseph that she loved. She looked at her little sister, blooming into such a beauty, and she hoped that she would have a young, handsome husband.

"You'll love your husband and be faithful to him, no matter what color eyes he has," she said, stroking Ihat's long, glossy hair.

Manasseh looked in every way like a boy of Egypt, but Ephraim was a curiosity. His eyes were much like his father's, but somehow softer and lighter in color, with long, curling lashes. It was, however, his hair which made him stand out against the black heads of Egypt. Joseph had it carefully clipped around the sides and back, but the top was a mop of golden curls. The child's every expression was adorable, and Asenath enjoyed listening to his childish babble and watching the light in his beautiful little face.

Near the close of the seventh inundation since Joseph became vizier of Egypt, an urgent message came to Asenath from On. She sent a servant to the palace to find Joseph. When the door opened she threw herself into his arms, weeping.

"Something terrible has happened to Niki! We must go to On at once!"

CHAPTER 8

"Through wisdom is an house builded; and by understanding it is established." Proverbs 24:3

Nikansut lay on his back. His glazed eyes stared at the ceiling. He did not move his arms or legs. When broth or drink were poured between his lips, he would not swallow, but the liquid ran out upon his bed.

Nofret and Ihat, accompanied by the wives of several priests of the Temple of Ra, wept and grieved his sad estate. Physicians and magicians from the court of Pharaoh labored over him. Asenath could get no answers from anyone in the house, so she and Joseph went to the Temple of Ra.

There the priests of Ra gathered about a stone table covered with a fringed cloth. On the table was a decayed corpse of a man, the linen embalming wrap tattered and quite fragile with age. A young priest who stood guard saw Joseph and Asenath approach and thrust a two-headed spear across their path.

"You are not allowed," he said.

Asenath looked past him and called, "Papa! It's me, Asenath. What happened to Niki, Papa?"

Potiphera looked up. He spoke to a priest, who brought a basin, and he washed his hands. He wiped them on a towel and spoke to the other priests, who nodded and continued their task.

Potiphera ushered Asenath and Joseph quickly out of the room into a small chamber to the left.

"Papa," Asenath repeated, "what happened to Niki?"

Potiphera shook his head sadly, and Asenath noticed the deep creases on his face and the bleary redness of his eyes.

"Niki passed the Third Grade, Melanephoris with great honor and jubilation," Potiphera said cheerlessly. "He received the golden crown from the hand of Apepi, which he dutifully threw down and trampled. When he was struck by Apepi with the sacrificial axe, he acquitted himself bravely. He endured the wrapping in the bandages of a mummy and received his instructions fearlessly."

"Then what, Papa?"

Potiphera sighed. "It was the grade of Chistophoris. Everyone in the Society believed Niki strong, and ready to take the vows of the Fourth Grade. I was there as he was armed with a sword and buckler and led blindfolded through terrors up the ascending passage and along the corridor to the first hall of the Great Pyramid. Apepi sat with me to oversee the ceremony."

"The chanter praised Niki for his courage and resolution. The Komastis, or Steward, handed him the cup of blood bittered with herbs. He drained it all. He was ornamented by various initiates. Apepi gave to him the buckler of Isis and covered him with the hooded mantle."

"All had proceeded well. Great excitement filled the hall, for all initiates knew the next order of business. I, myself, presented to him a scimitar with a jewelled grasp. With great ceremony we led him back along the corridor from the first hall to the juncture with the ascending passage. There Niki was instructed that he must descend the shaft and strike the head off the one he found in the grotto, and bring the head to Pharaoh."

Asenath gasped, but quieted as her father continued.

"He was pushed through the jagged opening of the shaft, which plunges almost vertically into the grotto. We heard his body thud against the rough walls of the shaft, but never a cry escaped his lips. I must tell you, that as his father, I was feeling very proud."

"What or who was in the grotto, Papa?"

Potiphera looked at her morosely. "A woman. She is the symbol of Gorgo, the spouse of Typhon, Assassin of Osiris. To avenge evil, Niki must grasp her hair in the darkness and strike off her head with the scimitar."

Asenath shuddered. She had long realized how horrible

initiation to the Mysteries was. Her father, her grandfather, indeed all the priests of Ra were initiates of the Mysteries. Yet, each time it was repeated, the horror of this deplorable deed astounded her.

Potiphera continued. "We could hear a scuffle down below, a shriek, a grunt, and then silence. Then we heard the shuffling of Niki's climb along the rough shaft to the top. He emerged triumphant, and lifted his bloody trophy to Apepi."

Potiphera bowed his head. His words became heavy and hard to hear. "Then it happened. Niki looked at the head of the woman that he held in his hand, and he turned to stone. We had to carry him from the Temple Pyramid. He has not moved or spoken since."

Asenath's heart ached for her brother. For gentle Niki to be compelled to decapitate a woman was repulsive. She could not grasp the information she had heard, for its horror.

"The woman for sacrifice comes usually from captives taken by our armies from distant places," Potiphera continued. "But Niki's sacrifice was not. The priest who gave his daughter in sacrifice to Osiris had great and profound vows. He depended upon Osiris to answer these weighty requests in exchange for his daughter. He grieves now, for her sacrifice was meaningless."

Asenath's heart sank. A dark dread seized her and she clutched her father's arm. "What priest was this, Papa, and who was his daughter?"

Potiphera looked at her, comprehension dawning upon his sorrowful features. "The priest is Sahure. His daughter was Ismala."

Asenath fell against Joseph with a cry, burying her head against his chest. He put his arm around her protectively.

"What do you do in the Temple?" Joseph asked, nodding toward the corpse.

"We dissect the corpse of an ancient priest. Perhaps we will find an answer in his dusty remains for the appalling events of this day. I must go back." Potiphera turned and shuffled away.

Joseph returned to Memphis, but Asenath and the boys remained at On. The physicians finally admitted that there was nothing they could do. The magicians shook their heads and returned to the palace of Apepi. Potiphera and the priests of Ra labored hard over the remains of the ancient priest, but no answer was found.

"Papa," Asenath said as she and Potiphera sat together. "You do know why Niki is as he is." She watched him and waited.

"I don't understand why the gods allowed Niki to slay the woman he loved. Never has it been done before."

"Will he get better, Papa?"

"I don't know." The shoulders of the great man trembled and he fell on his knees on the floor in weeping. "I don't know, I don't know," he cried repeatedly.

Asenath knelt at his side, and put her arm around his shaking shoulders. "Papa," she whispered. "You are the high priest of Ra. Surely he will hear your prayers. Surely he will bring Niki back for your sake."

Her father did not respond, but continued to sob out his sorrow, clutching his daughter to him.

Asenath stayed at Nikansut's side for hours at a time, speaking to him, stroking his arms and legs, trying to get him to swallow nourishment, but there was no change.

"Without food and drink he will die," Nofret said, her voice strained and tired. She sat beside her son, stroking his hair back from his gaunt face. She was cried dry of all tears, but her heart continued to break.

Suddenly she looked up at Asenath. "Your father has prayed to our gods. He has prostrated himself before them, offering whole herds of cattle and goats. He has cut himself and burned himself, but the gods have not answered him. He is the priest of Ra!" she cried. Then she calmed. "Perhaps the God of your husband could help our Niki."

Asenath's heart did not rebel against her mother's words. It was true that the gods of Egypt would not waken Niki. Joseph loved and trusted his God so completely. Perhaps He would answer Joseph's prayer for Niki.

The small reed boat was pushed along quickly against the current of the Nile from On to Memphis. Asenath ran along the columned streets to the palace. She demanded admittance and was brought before Apepi.

The Pharaoh smiled and his green eyes danced as he watched the wife of his vizier hurry toward him and fall in obeisance. He rose from his throne and took her hands, lifting her to her feet. Asenath," he greeted. "To what do I owe this honor?"

"Where is Joseph? We need him desperately at On."

"Is your brother still ill?" Apepi asked her.

"Yes, Your Eminence. Do you know where Joseph is?"

"He prepares the seed for the planting."

"Where?" she asked, impatiently.

"The granaries of Memphis, at the desert."

"Thank you," Asenath said as she hurriedly bowed away.

Accompanied by two of her father's servants, Asenath rode in a swift chariot to the granaries. Joseph spoke with several men who gathered beneath the shade of a grain tower. Asenath jumped from the chariot and ran through the burning sand to his side. He was mid-sentence, but she grasped his arm. He looked at her puzzled as she blurted out, "My mother wants you to come to On and pray to your God for Niki."

Joseph excused himself from the men, instructing them to continue without him. He got into the chariot with Asenath. As they flew over the desert sand to the river, Joseph held Asenath close so he could be heard above the rushing wind.

"I have been praying for your brother, Asenath. God can heal him. But God does not always do what we want. God has a higher purpose."

"What could be His purpose in Niki's death?" she

screamed. Joseph nodded, pulling her closer as she wept.

Joseph asked that the weeping and wailing cease in Nikansut's room. The women either left the room or quieted to sniffing as Joseph knelt at the bedside of his brother in law.

"There is no magic in prayer to Jehovah," Joseph told Nofret. "I will pray in faith to the One Who can heal Niki. I will trust in His will."

Even the sniffing hushed as Joseph lifted his eyes to heaven and spoke to His God. The occupants of the room all prayed daily to their gods of stone, but none had ever before heard a prayer like the one that Joseph lifted to the Lord. It was clear to all that Joseph knew His God and trusted Him implicitly.

When the friends had gone, Joseph stayed at Nikansut's side, speaking quietly to him. Asenath sat on the floor beside him.

"I've never had a loss like yours," Joseph was saying softly to Nikansut. "But I have known loss. And I also know the Lord God, the Creator of Heaven and earth. He is kind, and compassionate. His love can heal a broken heart. The Lord wants you to trust in Him, Nikansut. He wants you to let Him take away the pain you know, and give you peace in its place. Give it to the Lord. Trust in Him."

Joseph sat talking to Nikansut for hours. Asenath leaned against the bed and fell asleep. When she awoke, she and Joseph lay on a bed in a room of her parents' house. Joseph slept beside her, so she quietly slipped from the bed and made her way through the early morning light to Nikansut's room, where a servant sat watching.

Asenath sat on the edge of Nikansut's bed and stroked his hand. His hand was soft and relaxed, not rigid. She looked at his face, and his eyes were closed in sleep. She couldn't dare fully hope, but she sat, watching the gentle rise and fall of his chest as he slept peacefully. At last the room brightened and the sun peeped over the horizon and into the eastern window. The house began to stir with activity.

The hand Asenath held quivered and closed upon her fingers. Nikansut's eyes fluttered and opened with life, no longer glazed with unbearable pain. "Natha," he said.

"Niki!" she cried, embracing him. Then she shouted for the family, the household, to come.

The priest of On was happy at his son's recovery, but puzzled. When Nofret at first saw her son sitting on the edge of his bed, in his right mind, she earnestly contended to her husband that Joseph's prayers to his God had been answered. Potiphera had no explanation, for the gods of Egypt had turned a deaf ear to his pleadings for his son.

As Joseph and Asenath rode along the shining waters of the Nile to Memphis, Asenath sat at her husband's side, quietly considering the recovery of her brother. Nikansut was weak from hunger and sorrowing still over the death of his beloved, but he was awake, back from the edge of death.

"Was it your prayers to your God that healed my brother?" she asked Joseph.

"I prayed in faith, Asenath, and it was the Lord God who healed him."

"Why?" she asked. "Niki is an initiate to the Mysteries of Egypt's gods. Why did your God help him, when Egypt's gods wouldn't?"

Joseph's aqua gaze was kind as he spoke in words so gentle that she could almost imagine that they were spoken in love. "The Lord God loves your brother, Asenath, just as He loves you, and all of your family. I am happy that the Lord's mercy was shown to Niki." He paused. "Did you know that Niki will not continue in the Mysteries?"

Asenath only shook her head.

"Niki spoke with me. He wishes to move to Memphis, where he can learn from me about Jehovah, God of Heaven and earth. I will have need of a reliable scribe to keep the accounts when the time of famine begins and I must disperse the stored grain. Niki is well suited, for he reads and writes fluently. It is his desire to begin training for the position of scribe. As soon as he is strong enough, he will move to Memphis."

Manasseh, with Ephraim toddling unsteadily beside him, edged closely against Joseph's knee. He looked up into his face and said, "Pippa cried. I heard him, Papa. He cried because his gods wouldn't listen to him. But our God listened when you prayed, didn't he Papa? Our God made Uncle Niki well."

Joseph smiled and gathered his sons onto his lap. "Yes," he smiled to them both. "Our God made him well."

Manasseh turned sad eyes to his mother. "We wish that our God was your God, too, Mama. Our God can do anything."

Asenath turned her eyes away from her son and watched the dazzles of the sun upon the water. Never had she been so confused. Never had she been so certain that a prayer had been answered, yet the answer had come from Joseph's God! Not even fear of retribution from Egypt's gods could keep her mind true to them. They had failed, and Joseph's God had performed.

****

"This is the last harvest," Joseph told Asenath as they leaned against their balcony watching the city glimmer below them in the sunlight. "The river will not overflow the banks this year as it has done for seven years. There will be no rich harvest next year; there will be no harvest at all."

Asenath stood beside her husband and considered his words. Always she had been quick to oppose him. But since the healing of Nikansut, his words carried more weight with her than ever before. Perhaps it was true. If indeed a famine came, what then? Could she continue to resist Joseph's pleas. She suddenly caught herself mid thought. She must not lose her faith in Egypt's gods. She would wait and see.

A squeal rose to them from the garden, where Nikansut romped with his nephews. Asenath smiled. Nikansut had always been quiet and contemplative. Since he had come to live near them in Memphis, however, he exhibited an inner glow, a warmth of person. He spent many hours listening to Joseph speak about his God, his people, his history. He asked many questions and was always satisfied with the answers. The son of the sun god's priest had put his faith in Joseph's God.

Pharaoh Apepi, knowing that the seven years of plenty had come to a close, called his kingdom to a great festival. All who could leave their duties travelled to Memphis, and the city burst with humanity. The great festival lasted for seven days. Much was familiar to the citizens of Pharaoh's realm. The throngs crowded close to the stone paved streets to watch lengthy parades of foot soldiers, marching twelve abreast. Behind them came the iron chariots, the gold capped wheels flashing, the silver trimmed harnesses of the steeds glittering in the sun.

There was much about this festival, however, that was unfamiliar to the Egyptians as well. The usual display of Egypt's gods, carried on palanquins and attended by the priests, was not there. The naked dancers accompanied by lively musicians were not present. The sacrifice of hundreds of beasts before the altars of Apis and Ptah were not a part of the festival.

Joseph had asked his king to delete these things from the festival, for it was in honour of his God, who had brought to Egypt the years of great plenty. Apepi, willing to oblige his vizier, had consented.

The Pharaoh himself, with Joseph at his side, was carried high above the swarming crowds on palanquins held aloft by long poles. Apepi smiled and waved to his subjects. Joseph smiled, also, but Asenath knew that his heart was grieved when the citizens fell before them, prostrating on the ground. The Pharaoh of Egypt was revered as the Horus on earth, and worshipped as a god. Joseph desired no worship, but wanted all the praise to go to his God.

Each day, after the grand parade, a feast was served in the palace for the overseers of the nomes, or districts, of the kingdom. Then Joseph would sit at the Pharaoh's side on thrones on the stone pavement before the palace, and the citizens of Egypt would pass before them in a steady stream, staring at the two great men. Apepi would smile and nod at his people, his green eyes sparkling.

"I am a god to them, Zaphnathpaaneah," Apepi said. "If the famine indeed comes, then you shall also be worshipped."

"Would to God that they would trust in the true and living God and worship Him."

Apepi slapped Joseph's knee good naturedly. "You think of nothing else, do you!"

"It is the desire of my heart that all men everywhere would love and trust the Lord God of Heaven and earth."

Apepi laughed aloud and slapped Joseph's knee again.

****

Sure enough, when the dormant period had passed and the New Year arrived, it did not bring with it the swollen waters of the Nile. No rains fell, and no crops could grow, for the waters of the Nile were insufficient to fill the canals to the fields.

Some of Egypt's citizens bowed before Joseph in adoration, not understanding, although he tried to explain that it was the Lord God, Jehovah, who had cut off the waters. Some came to Joseph seeking to know more about his God. Many, the persons of Apepi's court, and the priests of Egypt's gods, were skeptical. The religion of their fathers and the strength of the Mysteries bound their hearts to Egypt's gods.

The time had come once more that Joseph would offer a sacrifice to his God. Nikansut accompanied the family and many servants as they took their offering to the desert. There Joseph showed Nikansut how to construct a rough stone altar. He told Niki about Adam and Eve and their sin against God, and God's provision for them in a lamb's blood. He repeated the stories of Abraham, Isaac, and Jacob, and the great promise of God to them of Messiah, the One who would someday come to defeat God's enemy with His own blood. The stories were familiar to Asenath, now, she had heard them so often. Somehow, standing there in the desert watching the proceedings, she felt a connection with the stories Joseph told.

Then Joseph deftly slit the throat of the lamb, catching its blood in a bowl. When at last the lamb burned on the altar, the two men knelt together and prayed. Never before had Asenath wished to share in the sacrifice, but this time she found herself desiring to kneel with them, to better hear the prayers they lifted to Jehovah. Manasseh knelt beside his father, and she heard his childish soprano ring out in prayer, as well. Two year old Ephraim struggled against her tight grasp, and she let him down, and watched him toddle to his father's side and kneel on chubby knees. The servants who had come also knelt in prayer, for one by one they had placed their faith in Joseph's God. She alone stood, watching, apart from the worshippers. And she realized that the strange sensation was an ache in her heart.

Potiphera would not discuss the failure of the inundation with Joseph. He would talk about his growing and busy grandsons; he would speak of trivial matters. But he would not speak of the river, the weather, the lacking crops. Joseph did not remind him of his pledge to consider Joseph's God if famine came.

And famine did come. When the time came that the crops should be gathered in from the fields, and there were no crops to harvest, Egypt's people came to Joseph to buy food. A storage bin was opened, and with Nikansut at his side marking clay tablets carefully with all transactions, Joseph fed Egypt.

Asenath's life did not change with the coming of the famine. There was always food and comfort in their home. Even with the distribution of grain Joseph rested every seventh day. Every morning Asenath faithfully brought her food offering to Isis as well, bowing before her gods.

"O Queen of Heaven!" she implored. "Why do you sit

idly by and allow Joseph's God to receive credit for the years of plenty, and now for bringing famine to Egypt? Put down Joseph's God and prove yourself to your people." Asenath searched the stone face of her goddess, but there was nothing, not a glimmer of response.

Asenath purchased a golden ankh, the symbol of the sun god, Ra, and hung it about her neck on a golden chain. She did not consciously consider why, but she hoped to keep Egypt's gods closer to her heart with the golden amulet.

Manasseh was six years old, and of age to attend the temple school to learn reading, writing, ciphering, and history. Joseph did not want his son to study the religion of Egypt, which was part of every Egyptian boy's schooling, so a tutor was hired, who came to the house daily to instruct Manasseh, carefully avoiding any reference to the gods of Egypt.

The tutor, whose name was Nepali, soon learned from the small son of Egypt's vizier that Jehovah, the Creator of heaven and earth, had caused the famine. He was taught by his eager instructor that Egypt's gods were powerless lumps of stone, and that only the true and living God could answer prayers. Manasseh told him the story of his uncle's illness and how God had raised him up.

And Asenath listened to the childish chatter of her son, too. He spoke with unblemished faith in his father's God. Asenath's doubts increased as time slipped away and it was evident to all that no such famine as this had ever before afflicted the land of Egypt.

Even the priests of Ra, the sun god, must come before Joseph to buy food. The fields of the sun would grow no more food than any in Egypt. Of necessity the offerings to the gods were scanty, but not forsaken.

And then came the peoples from other lands, by the hoards, into Egypt. Apepi, himself, came to the opened storage bins in Memphis to speak with his vizier. If grain were sold to the hungry of other lands, would the food last the seven years for

Egypt's own? Yes, Joseph assured him, the Lord his God had blessed Egypt's yield sufficiently to feed all who came. All who came bearing money to pay, Apepi reminded him, and went away counting the gain in his mind.

"Now that Niki is no longer in the Mysteries," Ihat mourned to her sister, "Papa has remembered that he must find a husband for me. Have you been praying to Isis for me to have a young and handsome one?"

Asenath had not, for her morning devotions were usually spent in hard questions to her goddess. She shook her head. "I don't know what good it would do," she heard herself saying.

"Then maybe if you prayed to the vizier's God, He would hear and answer."

Asenath looked at her sister astonished. There was no mockery in her face.

"He answered Joseph's prayer for Niki," Ihat said.

"But I don't know if He would answer a prayer of mine," Asenath told her.

"But will you try?"

"I have never prayed to Joseph's God."

"Well I think you should start," Ihat told her.

With his morning lessons completed, Manasseh sat with his brother on the floor playing with a wooden dog and a toy crocodile with movable jaws. The door opened and Joseph suddenly scooped both boys up into his arms, hugging them to him, and burying his face against them. He sat heavily upon a chair, still hugging them to him. They were startled, but submitted to his intense grasp. When his body shook with emotion, Manasseh called out to Asenath.

"Papa's crying, Mama!"

Asenath came to Joseph's side and put her hand on his arm. He looked up with a tear stained face, and eyes bright with tears.

"Joseph," she said gently.

"My brothers have come from Canaan to buy food."

Asenath knelt beside her husband so that she could better see his eyes. "Your brothers?" she queried. "The ones who sold you as a slave?"

"The very ones."

CHAPTER 9

"The wicked are overthrown, and are not: but the house of the righteous shall stand."Proverbs 12:7

Amazed, Asenath asked. "Did they know you?"

"I used an interpreter, and they could not have guessed that the man before whom they bowed was the brother whom they had sold as a slave."

"Your dreams," Asenath said, awed. "Remember the dreams that you told me about, in which your brothers bowed to you?"

"Yes, I remember." Joseph looked at her sadly. "I was rough with them. I spoke angrily, and I think even my translator was frightened. I accused my brothers of being spies. In defending themselves they told me that their father still lives."[17]

Joseph's body shook with emotion. The little boys clutched tightly in his arms squirmed. He released them and they slid off his lap, but crowded close to his knees beside their mother.

"If they are your brothers, Papa, isn't their father also your father?" Manasseh asked.

"Yes." Joseph said quietly. His eyes found Asenath's. "My father lives. And Benjamin also. He's at home with my father."

"Can we see your brothers?" Manasseh asked.

"No. They don't know who I am. I had them imprisoned at Potiphar's house. I told them that only one of them can return home, and that he must bring the younger brother to me, to prove that they are not spies."

Manasseh could talk of nothing else, but was strictly

---

[17] Genesis 42:6-12

112

ordered not to speak to Nepali about his uncles. It was difficult for him, for his uncles were the most exciting thing that had ever happened in his life. But he obeyed.

For two days the brothers of Joseph were imprisoned. Joseph went about his duties, but his mind was always on his brothers. The second evening he walked with Asenath in their flowered garden.

"If I send only one of my brothers home, he can't take all the grain that was purchased." Joseph's beautiful eyes, always sad since the coming of his brothers, seemed to plead with her for support. "My father and all my family would suffer. So I've decided to detain only one here in prison, and let the others take the grain to Canaan. I will tell them that they can come again for more grain only when they bring with them their younger brother."

Asenath nodded. "I think that's a wise decision. Which one will you detain here?"

"That's the hard part. Reuben and Judah both took my part when the others wanted to kill me. Reuben needs to return to my father, because as the eldest of his sons my father might trust him to bring Benjamin to Egypt."

"Who wanted to kill you?"

"All but Reuben and Judah."

"Whom shall you imprison then?"

Joseph stretched out eight fingers to Asenath. "Touch one," he said. She complied. "That is Simeon," Joseph said. "Simeon will stay here."

The next morning, after Joseph had left to speak with his brothers, Asenath wished to pray for him and the anguish of his soul. She descended to her small chapel, but could not bring her petition before Isis. Why should Isis care to help the vizier of Egypt as he faced his brothers, for he had never once bowed the knee before her? Asenath wandered away from the tiny chapel. Joseph spoke to his God everywhere. She glanced quickly about her to be sure that none could see her. She was uncertain of the position to maintain, for she had seen Joseph pray in many postures. So she merely stood beneath a date tree, hiding behind its slender trunk. Her eyes were open, but she focused only on the tree and directed her heart to Joseph's God.

"God of my husband," she said uncertainly. "I have never before spoken to You, and I don't know if You will listen to me. But if You will, please aid Joseph in this difficult task. Give him wisdom. He loves You. He would do anything to please You. Will You now mend his breaking heart and help him face his brothers?"

Asenath returned to the house and went about her duties there, but her mind could not forget her prayer to Jehovah. She had never felt assurance in her life as she did now, that a prayer of hers would be answered. What would Isis think? Asenath paused and reflected. Would Isis indeed care at all that she had prayed to Joseph's God? Isis had not as yet cared that Joseph's God received devotion as the One in control of the plenty and the famine.

Asenath waited at the front gate for Joseph to return that evening. When he came Nikansut was with him, and the two men entered silently.

Asenath greeted her brother and then asked, "How did it go, my husband?"

Joseph smiled wanly and took her hand as they walked to the house and mounted the steps.

"My brothers were fearful as they stood before me today. When I told them that one of them would remain while the others took the grain to Canaan, they trembled with fear. They didn't know that I could understand them as they spoke to each other."

They entered the house and sat as servants served them. When the servants had been sent away, Joseph continued.

"They spoke to each other about what they had done to me! They said that this distress has happened to them because they saw my anguish and wouldn't hear my pleadings when they sold me as a slave. Reuben defended himself by reminding them that he had told them not to sin against me, but they hadn't heard. They believe me to be dead." Joseph's blue green eyes were rimmed in red as he looked at his wife. "I couldn't help myself, I had to get away from them and weep. After all these years they feel remorse for what they did to me!"

"Perhaps only because they're in trouble, now," Asenath said.

Joseph nodded. "I had Simeon tied up before their eyes and taken back to the prison." He looked at Nikansut. "Then I ordered Niki to put every man's money into the top of his sack of grain.[18] And they left. Now I must wait until the grain runs out and they return for more. They know that they can purchase no more unless they bring Benjamin with them."

Asenath knew that Nikansut prayed to Joseph's God, too. So she looked at both the men and shyly said, "I prayed today for you, to your God, Joseph."

The room was silent. Joseph's eyes searched hers. Nikansut spoke first.

"Do you also trust in Jehovah?" he asked.

"I couldn't pray to Isis to help Joseph with his brothers."

"Do you trust in Jehovah?" Nikansut repeated.

Asenath faced him. "I believe that He has proven Himself to be a God. Joseph trusts Him. If He heard my prayer, then I knew that He could help Joseph."

This time Joseph spoke. He took Asenath's hand and his beautiful eyes were near tears once more. "Do you trust in Jehovah, yourself, Asenath?"

She faltered. Would she cease to pray to Isis and trust in Joseph's God, alone? No. Isis and Horus were her gods, and she could not desert them. But, yes, she believed that Joseph's God could hear prayer and would answer on Joseph's behalf. She looked at her husband in confusion.

---

[18] Genesis 42:17-25

"I believe that Jehovah is a God Who answers prayers on your behalf." She paused, watching the hope gleam in Joseph's eyes. "But He is not my God. I must trust my gods." She watched the bright hope fade on her husband's face, and the sadness replace it.

When Asenath first went to the prison beneath the home of Potiphar, Captain of Pharaoh's guard, she caused a grand stir. She came bearing food and asked to speak with the prisoners. Potiphar himself led her through the stench of the dungeon and allowed her to speak with a man imprisoned in a tiny cubicle. She gave him food and spoke kindly to him.

"Where is the prisoner from Canaan?" she asked Potiphar.

The captain of the guard called a young man to him. "Tavis can speak the Canaanite tongue," Potiphar told Asenath. "Perhaps the Hebrew will speak it also."

She was shown the man's cubicle. There she saw him, Simeon, brother to her husband. His hair was darker than Joseph's, but his eyes were very much the same. His hair hung against his collar, and his beard was full and long. He wore a long robe covered by a coat, and sandals on his feet. He sat dejectedly on a pile of animal skins and rags.

Simeon looked up startled to see a woman at the door. He stood to his feet. His eyes questioned her, but he remained silent.

Asenath had had no trouble talking to the other prisoner, but with Tavis interpreting, she found words difficult to her husband's brother. "I bring food for the prisoners, extras from our meal. Here." She held out the small basket of bread and dried fruit. He took it carefully and nodded to her.

"Thank you, kind lady," he said.

She fled the prison. All day the memory of Simeon's haunted look clung to her mind. She would go again. She would take him other things to help his comfort. But he must not suspect that he alone was the object of her concern. She said nothing to Joseph about her venture.

Asenath was always careful to go to the prison directly after Joseph left from the midday meal, while the boys were busy with Nepali. She purchased a pallet and two linen blankets, but made sure to give gifts to several of the prisoners before she came to Simeon's cell and gave him the bedding. Three times a week she took food to the prison, supplementing the poor diet of several grateful men. And always Simeon. She hoped her ruse was successful, for he could not know why she cared to help him.

As she listened to the lonely, desperate men, she learned of their families, their crimes, their hopes. But it was the tale of Simeon alone that she yearned to learn. As the days passed he came to anticipate her visits, and soon relaxed in her presence and poured out his own story. Neither Tavis nor Simeon was fluent in the language of Canaan, but communication was possible.

"I worship a God not of Egypt," he told her one day. Her heart flip-flopped, but she stood serenely listening to him. "I believe the God of my people is chastening me." He looked at her intently, and she felt timid beneath his blue green stare. "I am innocent of wrong doing. I know that you are the wife of the vizier, and it was he who imprisoned me, but my brothers and I are not spies. I hope that my father will allow my younger brother to come. Perhaps then your husband will believe that we are true men."

"Years ago my sister was defiled by a prince in my country, named Shechem. My brother, Levi, and I deceived Shechem and his people and slew them all. He had treated our sister as an harlot and deserved to die. But our father was concerned that we had killed the innocent with the guilty, and feared reprisal from the other people of the land. They never rose up to punish us, but perhaps my God now does so." He looked at her with his intense gaze, and she turned away and

118

departed.[19]

Asenath longed to speak with Joseph of the things that Simeon had told her. But she was sure that if Joseph knew of her visits to the prison, he would make her stop.

"I miss my family so," Simeon told her one day. "I have two wives. One is of the land of Canaan, and our son is Shaul. My other wife is a cousin of mine from the land of Haran. We have five sons. Their names are Jemuel, and Jamin, and Ohad, and Jachin, and Zohar."[20] His eyes were sorrowful as he looked at Asenath. "Will I ever see them again?"

Asenath was in sudden discomfort. "Pray to your God," she told him quietly. "Ask Him to recover you to your family."

"And of what use is prayer? If my God chastises me, why would He hear my prayers?"

"Your God loves those who trust Him."

Simeon looked at her curiously. "I think that you trust my God better than I, kind lady," he told her. She quickly departed.

Joseph was greatly wearied each day as he returned from his work of doling out the grain of Egypt to those who came to buy. Asenath was sorry that she must keep her secret from him, but she must.

As the famine stretched into the second year, Joseph organized men to control wild beasts along the river. Driven from their seclusion in the wilderness by thirst and hunger, the beasts came to the river, where they were a threat to human life. Dead animals must be carted from the streets and riverside into the desert daily. Farmers bemoaned the loss of cattle as the dams often cast their young and left them to die. The hart and antelope of the wilderness also left their offspring helpless.

---

[19] Genesis 34

[20] Genesis 46:10

Because the river was rapidly diminishing, irrigation was outlawed. Indeed, nothing would grow anyway. And the steady stream to the granaries of Egypt never subsided, for Egypt fed a hungry world.

Notwithstanding the famine, Pharaoh Apepi must have his dinners of state as usual. And indeed in the palace of the king one would hardly know that a famine existed. Asenath left her sons in the care of their nurses and Zedek at home and accompanied Joseph to the banquet. As always, Joseph and Asenath sat upon the dais with Apepi and his queen. Asenath surveyed the guests and saw there her mother and father sitting with Potiphar and Hoptet. The Venerable Jash and his lovely young wife sat near the dais, and Nophtet smiled and waved to her. She nodded to her friend. They had seen very little of each other lately, and Asenath was quite comfortable with that.

When the meal had finished and the entertainment was commenced, Nophtet found her way to the dais and greeted the king. He smiled at her appreciatively and chatted gaily. Nophtet bowed to Joseph, asking coyly, "May I borrow your wife, O Great One? I desire to talk with her awhile."

Joseph nodded and looked at his wife. His gaze was a warning, but he would let her visit.

Nophtet led Asenath away from the throng to a quiet garden of the palace. Squeals of delighted childish laughter floated over the wall. Asenath wished she could go find her little brothers instead of talking here with Nophtet.

"I have missed you, friend," Nophtet pouted. She continued when Asenath did not reply. "I suppose you're far too busy with your philanthropic endeavors to have time for your old friend."

Asenath's eyes widened as she looked at Nophtet. "I have two children," she said defensively. "They demand most of my time."

Nophtet frowned. "But you have plenty of time to visit criminals in prison."

Asenath took a breath and bit her lip. If Nophtet knew, did everyone? Did Joseph?

"I only share our plenty in this famine."

"Three times weekly? O, come now, dear. I tried so hard to help you find a lover. Have you stooped to bed with a soldier of Potiphar's guard?" She clucked and shook her head.

Asenath was suddenly disgusted at the woman before her, but she tried to speak calmly.

"Perhaps all there is in life to you is to be unfaithful to your husband. Well, I love my husband and have never betrayed his trust. There is more to my life than satisfying my cravings. I truly go to the prison to ease the burden of those imprisoned there." She stared defiantly at her friend.

Nophtet shrugged her shoulders. "Well even a soldier would have been better than nothing. You've admitted to me that the vizier can't love you. It's up to you, dear, if you want to live that way." She squinted at Asenath. "This sudden interest in the prisoners of Potiphar's house is quite curious. Hoptet speaks of it often, for it puzzles her, too."

Ah, thought Asenath, that's how she knows. Most likely Hoptet has spoken of it to my mother, too.

"I only serve my gods," Asenath said.

"The gods of Egypt demand only sacrifice to themselves, never sacrifice for worthless criminals." She lifted one eyebrow. "Perhaps you sacrifice to the God of the vizier."

Without thinking Asenath answered, "Perhaps."

Nophtet nodded. "It was bound to happen," she said. "Does your husband now love you?" She smiled wryly and left Asenath alone.

Joseph and Asenath could not visit Potiphera and Nofret because of the press of Joseph's work. But when next her parents visited, the question was raised. They sat upon the roof garden munching dried fruits and bread as the servants waved large palm fronds above their heads.

Nofret leaned toward Asenath and said, "Hoptet tells me

that she sees you several times a week lately."

Asenath glanced quickly at Joseph and then away. She was found out and there was nothing she could do.

"Does she?" Asenath said, taking a large bite of bread and chewing slowly.

"Yes. She said that you bring food and gifts to the prison quite regularly and give them to the criminals there."

Asenath almost choked. What could she say? She did not look toward Joseph.

Finally she swallowed and answered, looking at her hands. "My husband was imprisoned there if you'll remember. I only share our abundance in this famine with those who suffer need there." She turned her eyes to her mother. "Not everyone there is guilty of a crime, you know. Egypt's vizier was unjustly imprisoned there." She knew her mother could not reply to the contrary. Nofret pursed her lips.

"That's a very kind thing for you to do."

Asenath nodded. Joseph said nothing about it, and she dared not look at him until her parents left.

"The Lord God of heaven and earth gave the land of Egypt seven years of great plenty," Joseph said to his father in law. "And now we have famine, just as the Lord told me. Will you trust in Him?"

Potiphera squinted at Joseph. He preferred not to discuss it, but had no choice. "I recognize that you and Niki credit your God with his recovery. I confess that I can't explain it, for the gods of Egypt failed me when I prayed to them. But can you understand, Zaphnath, that I am deeply involved in Egypt's Mysteries, and cannot forsake the gods of Egypt so simply?"

"Was it not the Mysteries that caused Niki's infirmities?" Joseph asked gently. "I understand your devotion to that which you've learned all your life. But the Lord God, Jehovah, shows Himself in power to you now, in this famine, and He desires your trust in Him alone."

Potiphera's gaze held sadness, but his response was

unyielding. "I cannot, Zaphnath."

"Thank you," Joseph said to Asenath as they stood atop their balcony watching the Priest of On and his family depart with their entourage of servants.

Asenath turned toward him. "For what?"

"For visiting my brother, Simeon, in prison, and caring for his needs."

She was quiet for a moment. "How long have you known?"

"Since the first day that you went." His eyes smiled. "You could have spoken with me about it. I wouldn't have stopped you."

"I thought perhaps that you would want him to suffer as you had in prison and wouldn't care for me to make his way easier."

Joseph took her shoulders in his hands. "Do you know me no better than that?" he asked.

"Yes," she whispered. "You would not wish evil on anyone. But perhaps you wouldn't wish your wife to go to such a place."

"True. I wouldn't want you there at any other time. It's a horrible place. But I guessed that you did it for Simeon. Thank you," he said again.

Asenath stood looking into her handsome husband's beautiful eyes and smiled. "Please love me," she begged in her heart only. "Joseph," she said aloud. "I must confess that I am confused about my gods."

Joseph's eyes widened.

"I have prayed every day of my life to Isis. You know that I still do, every day. Yet, more and more I also desire to speak to your God. I can't explain it, but somehow I feel that my prayers to your God are heard, and I don't always feel that way when I pray to Isis." She saw the light of hope in his eyes, so she hurried on. "But I know that your God requires devotion to Him alone, and I still trust the gods of Egypt. I must, Joseph. Like my father, I have trusted them and prayed to them too long to simply forsake them. Does your God indeed hear my prayers since I pray also to Isis?"

Joseph smiled and sighed, nodding his head. "Yes, Asenath, God hears your prayers. Your petitions to Egypt's gods are to idols of stone. When you pray to God you speak to the true and living Creator of all. He loves you. He hears your prayers."

Joseph folded her in his arms and held her against him. "I pray that you will someday put all your trust in Him," he whispered against her hair.

Now that Asenath's private trysts were no longer a secret, she spoke to Joseph of the many things that Simeon had disclosed to her. He would sit and weep openly before her as she spoke to him of his family in Canaan.

"I pray every day that my brothers will soon return and bring Benjamin. I pray every day that I might also see my father again someday. I do trust the Lord God, Asenath. I believe He will answer my prayers."

Asenath stroked Joseph's golden hair. "I, too, believe that your God will answer your prayers." Joseph smiled at her.

Asenath sat with needlework in her lap and listened as Manasseh and Ephraim recited their lessons to Nepali. A servant scurried past her and soon Zedek approached and bowed low before her.

"Madame," he said, "the Master has sent for me."

"Go, then," she told him, rising from her seat and letting the needlework fall to the floor. She followed him to the door and watched him go. Why, she wondered, would Joseph call Zedek to the granaries?

Zedek returned before long, and with him were several men dressed in long robes, and wearing beards. Servants led their donkeys away to the stables to be fed.

Zedek hurried up the stairs and announced to Asenath, "The Master said that he will dine with these men, here, today at noon."

Joseph's brothers were there!

CHAPTER 10

"In the house of the righteous is much treasure: but in the
revenues of the wicked is trouble."
Proverbs 15:6

A senath dismissed Nepali, and he could not hide his curiosity as he passed the strangers in departing. The men stopped at the door, and for Asenath's sake Zedek translated as Reuben spoke to him.

"O sir, we came down the first time to buy food, and when we arrived at an inn and opened our sacks, every man found his money in the mouth of his sack. We've brought the full weight of that money back again. We also have other money with which to buy more food. We don't know who put the money into our sacks."

"Don't be afraid," Zedek told them. "Your God, and the God of your father, gave you the treasure in your sacks. We received your money."

The men hesitantly entered the room carrying large parcels, and as soon as the door was closed, a knock sounded. Zedek opened the door, and there stood Simeon, brought to Joseph's house by a guard of the prison. His hair and beard were long but orderly, for Asenath had taken to him a comb in prison. His clothes were soiled and worn. His brothers stared at him for a moment and then each fell in turn upon his neck with kisses and greetings.

Zedek ushered the men into the dining room. They stood awkwardly looking about them. It was then that Simeon saw Asenath. He approached her and fell on his face before her.

"Kind lady," he said, with Zedek interpreting. "But for your kind ministrations to me in the prison, I would have perished."

Asenath nodded to him, and it came to her mind that

Joseph had languished ten years in that prison without kind ministrations.

Zedek ordered the dinner prepared and then showed the men where to sit. Servants came to them and removed their sandals and washed and dried their dusty feet. Nectars of fruits on small trays were placed on the lattice stands beside the men.

Asenath sat upon the dais and watched the proceedings. One of these men was Benjamin, she was sure, for ten men had come from Canaan. It was hard for her to determine which he was, for the long beards they all wore made age undistinguishable for her.

Manasseh and Ephraim had seen the troop of men enter the house and came shyly into the dining room. They saw their mother sitting upon the dais and scurried to her side,

"Are these men our uncles?" Manasseh asked.

"Yes, but they don't know that."

The boys looked at each other puzzled.

"I can't understand everything they're saying," Ephraim said as he climbed onto his mother's lap to watch the strange visitors. "But they're speaking Hebrew, the language of Papa's people."

Joseph and Nikansut entered the room with several other Egyptians. The ten men were instantly on their feet. They carried their parcels to Joseph and bowed themselves before him.

"Is your father well, the old man of whom you told me? Is he still alive?" Joseph asked them as they knelt before him, with Zedek interpreting.

Reuben answered him. "Your servant, our father, is alive and in good health."

Then Joseph saw Benjamin. "Is this your younger brother, of whom you told me?" Joseph motioned for the men to stand and approached Benjamin. "God be gracious unto you, my son," he told Benjamin.

Asenath heard the tremor in Joseph's voice and stood to follow him as he quickly left the room and entered their bedroom. She handed the two boys to servants to care for and she closed the bedroom door. Joseph fell at the bedside and wept. Asenath knelt beside him and put her arms around him. Joseph suddenly clutched her, crying softly against her, "My brother lives! And he is here, in our house!"

"Your God has answered your prayers," Asenath told him gently as his body trembled with emotion. Joseph hugged her tighter in agreement.

When at last Joseph was able to control himself, he washed his face. Then he returned to the dining room and sat upon the dais with Asenath at his side. Nikansut and several other Egyptians were seated separately from Joseph's brothers. Joseph ordered the meal to be served and then spoke with Zedek, who rearranged the men in their seats according to age at Joseph's direction. Asenath saw the men marvelling at their seating arrangement. Servants brought bowls of warm water and towels for the men to wash their hands. As the trays of fine fare were brought into the dining room, Joseph ordered a special tray, containing five times the food of all the rest, to be placed upon Benjamin's lattice stand.

The men were cautious at first, for they were greatly puzzled at eating the noon meal with the vizier of the land, who had accused them of spying. But as they tasted the food and drank the sweet juices, they relaxed and talked freely among themselves, unaware that Zaphnathpaaneah, vizier of Egypt, understood every word that they spoke.

Asenath watched the brothers of her husband eat with hearty appetite, but she could not swallow the food. These were truly Joseph's brothers. Joseph's God had answered his prayer. His brother Benjamin sat there, before them, eating his large meal. Even the dreams that Joseph had dreamed as a young man had been from Joseph's God, for she herself had seen these men bow before him. The coming of the famine as Joseph's God had told him, had brought with it doubt about the gods of Egypt. The coming of Joseph's brothers now brought a curious wonder about Joseph's God. Was He the Almighty One, as Joseph said? Were the gods of Egypt powerless idols of stone, and Jehovah alone God?

As the meal was finished, servants again brought the small bowls of water and towels for the hands. Joseph called Nikansut to him.

"Fill the men's sacks with grain, as much as they can carry, and put every man's money in his sack's mouth," Joseph told him. "And put my silver cup in the sack of the youngest with his money."

Zedek escorted the men to an inn with their donkeys and provided provender there for the animals.

Joseph did not return to the granaries for food distribution that day. He and Asenath sat in the dining room and opened the parcels brought from Canaan. In the packages they found balm, spices, and myrrh, nuts, almonds, and a little honey. Joseph wept again, for this present from his father to Egypt's vizier was a sacrifice in time of famine.

When Asenath awoke the next morning Joseph had already risen. She called her maids to dress and groom her quickly, and forgetting her devotions to Isis, she sought Joseph. He stood on the balcony, watching toward the north.

Asenath stood at his side silently. She squinted into the first rays of the sun as it lifted its golden head over Memphis. A low murmur in the city about them grew into the thrum of everyday business.

"Zedek went to the inn to send my brothers away at first light," Joseph said.

Asenath strained to see if she could detect ten long robed men leading donkeys away from the city to the north. She could not. They stood silently on the balcony as the sun rose higher, and finally Zedek returned.

As soon as he had mounted the stairs and stood before his master, before he spoke a word, Joseph told him, "Take twelve men on horses with you and follow them. When you catch them, say to them, 'Why have you rewarded evil for good? In stealing my master's divining cup you have done evil.'" Zedek bowed before Joseph and quickly departed.

Asenath wanted an explanation, but dared not ask. Joseph continued to lean against the balcony rail, watching northward. The servants, unsure about their master's behavior, offered trays of fruit and bread, but Joseph declined. Asenath thanked them and sent them back to the kitchen with the food.

An official from the granaries came hesitantly to ask after Joseph. Joseph told him that a pressing matter kept him away today, and that Nikansut, his scribe, would handle the dispersement of grain. The man departed, and still Joseph waited, with Asenath at his side.

Manasseh and Ephraim finished their breakfast and came outside to play in the yard below the balcony. When Nepali came for their lessons, Joseph excused him for the day.

Asenath felt Joseph go rigid at her side and he released a long sigh. She looked where he was watching, and she saw Zedek and his twelve men on horses escorting Joseph's brothers and their donkeys back to Joseph's home. They entered the gate with shuffling steps and heads hung low. Leaving their donkeys to the servants, they approached the house.

Joseph and Asenath descended the stairs. As the men approached, they all fell prostrate before Joseph. Asenath noticed that their clothing had been torn and hung in shreds from their bodies.

Joseph spoke harshly to the men, as Zedek translated. "What did you think you were doing? Didn't you know that a man such as I can ascertain such things?"

Joseph's brother, Judah, looked up at him from his prostrate position and said, "What shall we say, my lord? What can we speak? How shall we clear ourselves? God has found out the iniquity of your servants. We are your servants, both we, and he with whom your cup was found."

Joseph spoke a word and Zedek commanded the men to

stand upon their feet.

"God forbid that I should make you all my servants," Joseph told the men. "Only the man in whose hand my cup was found shall be my servant; the rest of you may go to your father in peace."

Judah stepped boldly forward, coming quite near to Joseph. "Oh, my lord, I beg you to let your servant speak a word in my lord's ear, and don't be angry with your servant, for you are as powerful as Pharaoh."

Judah hurried on, with Zedek hastily interpreting. "My lord, you asked your servants, 'Do you have a father or a brother?' We told you, my lord, that we have an old father and a younger brother, the child of his old age. His brother is dead, and he alone is left of his mother, and his father loves him. And you said to your servants, 'Bring your youngest brother down to me, that I may see him with my eyes.' We told you, my lord, that he couldn't leave his father, for if he should, his father would die. You told us that unless we brought our youngest brother to you, we could no longer see your face, or purchase grain. When we returned to our father, we told him your words. When he commanded us to go again to buy more food, we reminded him that unless we took our youngest brother we could not see your face. With great sorrow our father grieved over the first son of his beloved wife, whom he believes to have been torn in pieces by wild animals. He told us that if we brought our youngest brother to Egypt, and he came to any mischief, we would cause our father's gray head to go in sorrow to the grave."

Judah took a deep breath and plunged on even more fiercely. "When I return to your servant, my father, without his youngest son, because his life is bound up with his son's life, my father will die, and my brothers and I will be the cause of his death. I gave my word to my father that I would return his son, and I shall bear the blame for my father's death forever."

Judah fell upon his knees before Joseph, clasping his raised hands together. "I beg you, my lord, let me stay as your bondman and let my youngest brother return with his brothers. I can't go to my father without him, and see the evil that will come upon my father."

Asenath had listened intently to the words of her brother in law as he pled with her husband. But she had watched Joseph tremble, and when Judah had concluded his plea, Joseph was visibly shaken, battling for control.

"Cause every man to leave me!" he shouted to Zedek. The children were ushered quickly up the stairs by their nurses, and the servants melted away into their quarters. Only Joseph and Asenath stood upon the pavement with the ten Hebrew men.

Joseph wept aloud. Asenath had never heard such a sound. "I am Joseph!" he cried loudly in Hebrew. "Does my father yet live?"

The men were troubled, frightened at his announcement.

Joseph said, "Come near me. Please do." The men moved slowly nearer to him. He fought to control his voice and spoke again with more composure. "I am Joseph, your brother, whom you sold into Egypt."

The men cringed, and some cried out softly.

"Don't be grieved," Joseph said, almost tenderly, "don't be angry with yourselves that you sold me here, for God sent me before you to preserve life. The famine has been in the land these two years, and there are five more years in which nothing will grow or be harvested. God sent me before you to preserve you a posterity in the earth, and to save your lives by a great deliverance. So you see, it wasn't you who sent me here, but God. He has made me greatly trusted of Pharaoh, lord of all his house, and a ruler throughout all the land of Egypt."

Joseph's words and manner eased his brothers' fears. They all stepped closer, peering at his face, but said nothing.

"Hurry and go up to my father, and tell him that his son Joseph lives! Give him this message from me, 'God has made me lord of all Egypt. Hurry and come down to me, and you shall dwell in the land of Goshen where you can be near to me, you and your children, and your grandchildren, and your flocks and herds, and everything you have. I will nourish you here, for there are yet five years of famine. Otherwise you and your household will come to poverty.'"

Joseph looked intently at his brothers. "Your eyes see, and the eyes of my brother Benjamin," and Joseph smiled at Benjamin, "that it is my mouth that's speaking to you. Go tell my father of all my glory in Egypt, and of all that you've seen, and hurry and bring my father here."

Benjamin had approached to stand before Joseph, and suddenly the two men embraced, weeping. Then, one by one, Joseph embraced his brothers weeping, and kissed each one.[21]

All day and far into the night Joseph sat with his brothers in his house and talked. Asenath couldn't understand their words, but she heard the happiness in Joseph's voice, and watched the animation of his face. Manasseh and Ephraim crept to him and climbed upon his knees to watch the men and listen to the strange words.

The city of Memphis had heard Joseph's cry, and his weeping had reached to the palace of Pharaoh. The news soon reached Apepi that the brothers of Zaphnathpaaneah had come from their home. Apepi was delighted, and sent a messenger to Joseph.

The message from Pharaoh was such: "Tell your brothers to pack their beasts and return to Canaan. I will send wagons with them, and command them to bring their children and wives, and your father in the wagons to Egypt. Tell them that I will give them all the good of the land of Egypt, and they shall eat the fat of the land."

Joseph's brothers slept that night at Joseph's home. When the men had broken their fast in the morning, they accompanied Joseph to fetch the wagons and teams of oxen. Joseph gave each

---

[21] Genesis 44:1-45:14

of his brothers a change of Egyptian raiment. But to Benjamin he gave three hundred pieces of silver and five changes of raiment. He sent gifts to his father to be eaten on the trip to Egypt: ten donkeys loaded with delicacies of Egypt, and ten donkeys loaded with corn and bread and meat.

Asenath knew that her brothers in law were eager to leave and get back to their families in Canaan. They had exciting news and wondrous gifts, and they missed their loved ones. Simeon, in particular, was homesick. Joseph, too, wanted them to get going, for the sooner they left, the sooner they could return, bringing Joseph's father with them. Yet, Joseph hesitated to let them leave him, especially Benjamin, for he had at last been reunited with family. When everything had been loaded, and preparations were made, he had to let them go. Asenath and the boys went with Joseph to accompany them outside the city walls several miles to the north. They stopped on a rise from which they could watch the caravan of wagons descend to the delta and cross toward Canaan. The hot wind of famine blew Asenath's heavy tresses, and the relentless sun beat on their heads and backs, but they stood mutely still, watching his brothers until they disappeared into the horizon.

Joseph returned to the granaries of Egypt, but his heart went with eleven men on a long, weary journey to Canaan. A strange excitement knotted in Asenath's stomach. Joseph had prayed all his years in Egypt to see his father again. If Joseph's brothers indeed told their father, and if he would come, Joseph would once again see him. Joseph's God. Joseph's God. The thought rang between her temples daily. She went once to Isis, with the morning oblation, but her prayers seemed hollow, and Isis unmoved. She couldn't speak to Isis of Joseph's brothers and coming father, nor mention the famine which Joseph's God had promised, and there seemed nothing else of which to speak to Isis.

So, secretly, she avoided Isis and prayed to Joseph's God. She prayed that the ten brothers of Joseph would have a safe and prosperous journey to their homes. She prayed that Simeon's reunion with wives and children would be sweet. She prayed that Jacob, the old father of Joseph, would believe the report that Joseph was living still, and would come with his sons in the wagons of Pharaoh to Egypt; to Joseph.

It was the second week since Joseph's brothers had gone. Asenath was nursing a scratch on Ephraim's knee, when a servant announced a visitor. She delivered Ephraim to his nurse and went to the front gate.

A woman stood before her. Her sagging shoulders shook and tearstained eyes peered from a haggard face. Asenath hardly recognized Nophtet.

"Come in," she invited, and taking her friend's hand, she led her to the garden, and offered her a seat beneath a canopy. A servant lingered near, and Asenath ordered cool nectar and fans.

"You don't look well," Asenath said gently.

"And I am not," her friend answered mournfully. She sat listlessly, with her hands twitching in her lap. Suddenly she fell from her chair onto her knees and clutched Asenath's knees. "I have been discovered by the Venerable Jash to be an unfaithful wife!" she cried. She looked at Asenath with red, swollen eyes, her kohl smeared and running with her tears. "Oh, how I mocked your fidelity to the vizier! But you were wise, much wiser than I!" Her eyes grew large with her intensity. "You were right, too. It wasn't love that I found with the many men I had." She clutched more tightly to Asenath's legs. The servants came, and Asenath waved them back.

"You are the wife of the vizier. Help me!"

"What can I do?" Asenath asked.

"Plead for my life! The Venerable Jash designs to have me flogged and executed!"

CHAPTER 11

"Except the LORD build the house, they labour in vain that build it." `Psalm 127:1a`

A senath considered her friend. She deserved her fate for her sins against her husband. Yet, Asenath couldn't sit by and let her die without trying.

"I can do nothing without first speaking with my husband," she said.

"But the vizier will side with the Venerable Jash!" Nophtet cried. "He will only forbid you to plead on my behalf, and speak against me to my husband himself."

"My husband's God is a God of mercy. Therefore my husband is a man of mercy. He will listen to me. If he allows me to go to your husband, then I shall go."

Nophtet wept, "Thank you, thank you."

Asenath had briefly explained to Joseph and now waited patiently for his reply. She trusted him. She knew that if he forbad her to plead with the Venerable Jash on Nophtet's behalf, that he would be wise in his decision. Still, she hoped that she may speak to save her friend's life.

Joseph had pulled the heavy wig from his head, as was his custom on returning home in the evening. He scratched his head, his golden hair glowing in the lamplight.

"Your friend has sinned against her husband. The laws of Egypt allow a man to put his wife to the floggers."

"She'll die."

Joseph looked sadly into her eyes. "Why did you choose Nophtet for a friend?"

Asenath remembered. She had been young and lonely, and was feeling very sorry for herself that Egypt's vizier required such strange and hard things from her. He didn't want her to pray to her gods or drink beer. Nophtet had been a sympathetic

135

ear.

But she couldn't explain it to Joseph. "We became friends years ago," was her only explanation. "Will you let me speak to the Venerable Jash on her behalf?"

"And what will you propose that he do? The man's pride has been destroyed by his wife's infidelity. I know the man, and I don't believe he'll forgive his wife. He will demand satisfaction."

Tears came and Asenath's shoulders shook. "Then must Nophtet die?"

Joseph took her into his arms and held her against him. "What do you think of buying her as your slave?" he asked.

"Do you think the Venerable Jash will sell her to me?" she asked him hopefully.

"Perhaps. But you shall not go to him. I will ask him if he is willing to sell her as a servant for my wife."

Asenath pulled back from his tight clutch and looked into his beautiful eyes. "Will you, Joseph? Thank you." Strangely, she felt loved, even though she knew it couldn't really be so. But her love for Joseph was enough to satisfy her for the moment.

Asenath sat with her sons for their lessons. Nepali commented on how well Ephraim was learning his lessons, although only four years of age. Asenath knew that he had learned much just sitting in on Manasseh's lessons, and she also knew the constant instruction the older brother gave the younger.

"Who is the Creator of all things?" Manasseh would drill.

"The Lord God, Jehovah," came Ephraim's answer.

"What are the gods of our Pippa and Pharaoh?"

"They are idols of stone."

"Can they hear and answer our prayers?"

"No," the golden curls would shake, "only the Lord God can hear and answer our prayers."

At first Asenath had wanted to reprimand Manasseh for such recitation, and make him stop. However, she had suppressed that desire with another, that of hearing more about the God of Joseph. Her little boys trusted Him just as her husband did. She felt curiously envious of their faith in Him.

She was waiting for Joseph's return. He had gone to speak with the Venerable Jash. She tried to keep her mind off Joseph and listen as Manasseh recited his lesson. Suddenly a thought struck her. Pray. She should pray for Joseph, for Nophtet. She should pray that the Venerable Jash would listen and comply. She excused herself from the lessons and climbed up to the roof garden.

"God of Joseph," she began, "my husband says that You will hear my prayers to You, even though I have not renounced the gods of Egypt. I cannot go to my gods to plead for Nophtet. I don't think they would help her. But Joseph always tells me of Your great compassion, and I believe it is true. Will you help Joseph as he bargains with the Venerable Jash? Will you make the Venerable Jash willing to sell Nophtet to Joseph?" She paused. Joseph had said that the posture in prayer was not important. But it was to her, now, so she fell on her knees, and squeezing her eyelids tight against the bright sunshine she continued.

"I believe that You can answer my prayer, God of Joseph." She remained on her knees long after her prayer had ended. When she rose and walked about on stiff legs, assurance swept through her. Never had she felt such assurance when she had brought a petition before Isis.

Asenath was still pacing the roof when she heard her boys noisily greeting Joseph. She descended from the roof and waited for the boys to return to Nepali. Joseph reached a hand to her and they went to their room.

Joseph pulled his wig off, smiling. "You have a new lady's maid," he said. "Or put her to the kitchen, or even the fields, if you wish. She is yours."

Asenath threw herself into Joseph's arms. "Thank you!" she cried. Suddenly she stopped and looked into his smiling aqua eyes. "Did it cost you terribly much to purchase her?"

"The price of a slave is twenty pieces of silver." He paused. "That was my price,"[22] he said quietly. Asenath laid her head against his chest feeling the coolness of the golden chain about his neck, and hearing his heart beat. "But I offered the Venerable Jash one hundred pieces of silver. He was curious that I thought her so valuable. He cannot understand how even a woman could value her, now." Joseph paused again. Then he spoke into her hair. "He warned me that she may be a bad influence on my wife."

Asenath continued to lean against her husband, and the memories flooded her. Always Nophtet had tried to influence her to infidelity. How thankful she was that she had never fallen prey. But thankful to whom? Who had kept her from such trespass? Surely not Isis, for wanton exercise was only frowned upon if one was discovered in indiscretion. Was it her own strength that had spared her from heeding Nophtet's appeals? She knew that couldn't be, for she had always been most vulnerable when with her friend, baring her wounded soul in revealing the injustices of the vizier against her. She knew, as her heart beat against his, that the God of Joseph had kept her from indiscretion for Joseph's sake, because Joseph was His own faithful one.

"She will be my own personal maid," she whispered against him. "Your God has never allowed her to influence me before, neither shall she sway me now."

Joseph pulled her back quickly to see her face. He smiled hopefully. "Is my God your God?"

"I pray to Him, and He answers prayer. I prayed that He would let the Venerable Jash sell Nophtet to you. But I can't say that I trust Him as you do. I'm not willing to let go of Egypt's gods."

Joseph pursed his lips and nodded. "I'll keep praying for

---

[22] Genesis 37:28

you," he said. And Asenath knew he would.

Nophtet came that day, escorted by four soldiers. She had been bought with a price, and as chattel, she must be guarded safely to her new master. She brought nothing with her but the clothing she wore. Her head had been shaved, and she wore no make up.

When she entered the house, she fell on her face before Asenath. Asenath was unsure how she should proceed, for Nophtet was her friend. However, now she was mistress and Nophtet servant. She had many servants and was kind to all. But Nophtet knew her heart, her secrets.

"Rise, Nophtet," she said.

Nophtet raised her red, swollen eyes to meet her friend's. She rose to her feet, keeping her gaze on Asenath. "Thank you, Madame, for giving me the privilege of serving you."

Asenath placed her hand on Nophtet's trembling arm. "To purchase you as a servant was the only way to save your life. But you are my friend."

Nophtet bowed her head. "I will serve you willingly."

"Yes, and the service I most need is companionship."

Nophtet looked up through her swollen eyes with amazement. "Why?"

"You didn't wrong me," Asenath told her. "I hold nothing against you."

Asenath personally assigned Nophtet's quarters in the servant's living area in the first story of her house. She gave her a stack of fine linen dresses such as all the women servants wore which, like those of Asenath, fully covered the bosom. She gave her a short, thick wig of wool to cover her head until her own thick black hair grew again.

As the days passed Nophtet's discomfort eased as she accompanied Asenath through her days. She learned that her mistress seldom visited the tiny hidden chapel to pray to her gods. Along with the other servants she rested with the family of the vizier on Sabbath. She learned to eat the meals devoid of fish and vegetables. But she keenly felt the dearth of beer.

"You so much enjoyed beer when visiting me," Nophtet respectfully mentioned, wincing at her own reminder of her former days. "How do you manage without beer?"

"At first I believed I would die for lack of it," Asenath told her. "I drank it to the full whenever I could, at my parents' home, at the palace, with you. But as the years have progressed, and I have not drunk it here, in my home, I have lost my ardent desire for beer. I find the nectars and juices that my husband and I enjoy to refresh me well. And our style of living seldom causes me to wish for the sweet forgetfulness that beer affords. I surprise myself, sometimes, at the palace, to refuse the beer for juices."

"I shall miss it," Nophtet said sadly.

Early one morning Asenath saw a young servant man leaving Nophtet's quarters. She confronted her servant.

"Nophtet, while living in our home, you may not seduce the servants."

Nophtet's familiar smirk faded quickly, and she fell before Asenath, bowing before her on the floor.

"Please, Mistress," she begged, "don't send me away."

Asenath felt that the plea was more for show than of sincerity, but she didn't know how to handle her friend in this matter. She couldn't send her away, for that would mean eventual death for such a one as Nophtet.

Through everything, Asenath was ever mindful of Joseph's brothers. They would return, if their old father believed that Joseph still lived and would leave his own country and come to Egypt. She no longer made daily visits to Isis with offerings and prayers. But she found herself daily petitioning the God of Joseph for the return of Joseph's brothers, and the coming of his father. She was sure that Joseph prayed for this also, and fully believing that Jehovah would answer these prayers, she decided to visit her parents again before their arrival.

Nepali was relieved for the visit, and Manasseh and

Ephraim, accompanied by their nurses, went with Asenath to the city of On. Several servants attended them, among them Nophtet, who went as her companion.

The colossal Temple of Ra had always impressed Asenath with its grandeur and size, but somehow its splendor was dimmed as Asenath viewed it now. She hurried to the home of her parents and was warmly greeted by her mother and Ihat. Nofret frowned at Nophtet and whispered fiercely to Asenath, "Why is that woman with you?"

"She is my personal maid."

Nofret scowled. "She has been disgraced."

"She has lived disgracefully since I've known her, Mama, but was only recently discovered by her husband. Will you let her into your home for my sake?"

Nofret's frown remained, but she nodded. "For your sake, Natha."

Asenath turned to hug her sister and noticed the full bodiced dress she wore. Greatly puzzled, she followed her mother, as Manasseh and Ephraim ran to find their uncles. Ipi and Wehemki were young men of thirteen years, but they enjoyed the company of their young nephews.

The feet of the guests were washed and refreshments were brought. Asenath took a goblet of beer and sipped it, but found herself repulsed by the pungent brew. Nophtet, who stood behind her, sighed at the sight of the beer, but Asenath knew it would be improper to give the goblet to her maid. So she set the still full goblet on the small lattice stand at her side.

"I've ordered a boat to Giza," Nofret told her. "I feel a great need to pray to the spirit of Ipitoket." She paused. "Your father is greatly troubled these days. The people are questioning the gods because of the famine. Even a few of the priests of Ra have expressed their doubts to your father. The Enlightened Ones have been performing special sacrifices and rituals at the Great Pyramid Temple. Yet, the famine persists, and I fear for your father's health. He doesn't eat properly. He spends whole nights in petition before his gods." She turned troubled eyes to her daughter. "Perhaps the spirit of his own father can intercede with the gods."

Two boats transported the women, the boys, and the servants to the burial grounds of Giza. The grave Sphinx stared unheeding at their approach. Asenath once again felt her own insignificance in the presence of the massive gleaming pyramids.

At the river's expanding edge the petitioners smeared themselves with the thick black mud. They wound through the maze of tombs to the mastaba of Ipitoket. Inside the small room Asenath knelt with her mother before the image. The smooth, unfeeling stone face looked like her beloved grandfather, but there was no warmth in the gaze of the stone eyes. The women placed their offerings on the small altar before the image. In tears Nofret began to plead loudly to her dead father in law on behalf of her husband, who wasted away with the famine of Egypt. "Speak to the gods," she begged him. "Convince them to send the waters for the crops to grow, or your own son will die of grief and soon join you in the underworld." She cried on until the sun began to dip into the desert horizon.

Asenath had listened to her mother's pleas. When at last her mother silenced, she quieted her own weeping and spoke quietly, sincerely. "Pippa, please explain to the gods that the God of Zaphnathpaaneah, Vizier of Egypt, receives the recognition for bringing this famine upon us. And the vizier has predicted five more years of dearth. Pippa, tell the gods that they can relieve the doubts of Egypt's people by proving Joseph's God wrong. Tell them to send the plenty once again, and Egypt will believe and rejoice." She prayed to her dead grandfather's spirit hopefully. She was one among those who doubted the power of Egypt's gods. But her faith had not totally perished. She clung to the tenets of her religion precariously. And she had loved and trusted her grandfather. He had been the chief priest of Ra. Perhaps the gods would listen to him. Perhaps he could persuade them to act.

In a quiet whisper, Asenath moved her lips to add, "Pippa, I try to do as you counselled me before my marriage to the vizier. I try to venerate Egypt's gods and resist the God of Zaphnathpaaneah. Do you know my struggle, Pippa? Do you know the torment of my soul?" She waited prostrate before the stone image, but there was no answer, no solace.

Manasseh and Ephraim had sat obediently silent throughout the mourning and prayers. When his mother stopped speaking, Manasseh crept to his grandmother's side. He put his arms about her torso and hugged her as she lay prostrate. Nofret raised herself and embraced her grandson.

"Grandmother," he said. "Mama has told me what a wonderful man her Pippa Ipitoket was. But he is dead. He can hear and answer your prayers no more than the gods of Egypt can. Only the Lord God Jehovah can hear and answer prayers. And the famine cannot be removed, because He said that it would endure seven years."

Nofret did not speak. She continued to grasp the child close to her, so he spoke again.

"It was the Lord God who healed Uncle Niki when nothing else could save him. Uncle Niki trusts now in the Lord, and he is very happy, even though such a terrible thing happened to him." The wise child had been told the sad story by his uncle. "Grandmother, it has been told me that when Uncle Niki was very ill you asked for my father to pray to his God for him. Do you believe that my father's God can help my Pippa?"

Nofret trembled. She feared the very fact that she did believe such a thing. For she also feared the deities of Egypt, and their dreadful power.

"Your Pippa's illness is not like Niki's," she told the child. "He wastes away because he trusts his gods, and they won't speak to him."

"It doesn't matter the malady," Manasseh told her. "My God can heal any disease, even Pippa's. If Pippa would only trust in the Lord, his troubles would be over."

Asenath watched her mother's face in the dim flickering light of the mastaba. A battle was being fought, she knew, in her mother's heart. It was much like the war that was raging in her own.

Although much older than Manasseh, Ipi and Wehemki stayed at his side, asking questions, listening to his confident answers. They, too, pondered the failure of their father's gods to answer his pleas. They had no firm and certain faith in the gods of Egypt as their young nephew had in the God of the vizier. Nofret knew that her sons listened to Manasseh, but she did not stop them. If fact were known, she, too, would have sat at the child's feet to learn of his God.

When they had returned home, Nofret went to the kitchen to order the supper, and Asenath was left alone with her sister.

"Why do you dress so?" she asked Ihat.

"The vizier compels you to dress thus because he alone should set eyes upon your nakedness. So, I cover myself that none will see my nakedness." Tears suddenly filled her large black eyes. "I'm almost eighteen years of age. Papa has found me a husband."

Asenath smiled, beginning to congratulate her sister, but she stopped at the profound sadness in Ihat's visage. "Has he chosen someone horrible?" she asked.

"He's a young priest in the Temple of Ra."

"Then what's wrong?"

"I trust in the Lord God Jehovah, just as Niki does. My husband to be is a priest of Egypt's gods. I fear that we will never love and trust one another. We will live in two different worlds, like you and the vizier, and we'll never be happy."

Is Joseph unhappy? Asenath wondered. Always she had considered only her own unhappiness in Joseph's demands. She had always wanted him to love her although she knew his love for his God prevented it. But had he lived all his years with her in unhappiness? She could truly say that her first years with him had been ones of great distress for her because of her selfishness and stubbornness. But now, she admitted to herself, she was happy. Did Ihat see only Asenath's unhappiness of the past, or did she truly see that Joseph as unhappy? Asenath only wanted to return to Joseph, now. She wanted to know, needed to know. Was he unhappy?

When Potiphera, Priest of On, High Priest of the god Ra returned home for supper, Asenath was shocked at his gaunt appearance. His shoulders stooped, making him appear smaller, more frail. The strong, confident father she once knew stood before her now wasted in body and spirit. His eyes were hollow and sunken and his skin sallow. She understood her mother's great concern for him.

"Papa." Asenath greeted him gently, embracing him while trying to subdue her tears. She sat at his side as servants washed his feet.

"Your mother tells me that you prayed at Ipitoket's mastaba today," he said.

"We did. Papa, have you heard that Joseph's brothers came to Egypt to buy corn and he has sent them home to bring his father here?"

"Niki told us."

"Papa, when Joseph was very young he dreamed two dreams. In one the sheaves of grain of his eleven brothers bowed down to his sheaf. In another the sun and moon and eleven stars bowed to him."

"The vizier is an interpreter of dreams," Potiphera said with contempt. "What did these dreams mean?"

"Joseph can't discern dreams, Papa, it's his God who tells him the interpretations. He didn't know the meaning of his dreams when he was young. But when his brothers came from Canaan to buy grain they didn't recognize him, and I saw them bow before him on the ground, Papa, just as in his dreams. I believe his God was telling him when he was young that someday he would be lord over his brothers. And when I saw his dreams fulfilled, I knew that his God had done it."

Potiphera looked sadly at her. No anger remained in the tired face. "I have lost Niki and Ihat to Zaphnath's God. Have I lost you, too?"

"Papa, I've tried so hard to venerate only Egypt's gods. I've kept a temple to Isis, but my prayers to her seem useless." Asenath looked her father squarely in the eye and took a deep breath. "I do pray, sometimes, to Joseph's God, for I have seen Him answer prayer. He healed Niki. He brought Joseph's brothers. And now I pray to Him that He will bring Joseph's old father as well. I have not deserted my gods, but I have found Joseph's God to hear and answer prayer."

Potiphera did not answer his daughter. He only looked sadly upon her. Was his great sadness for her, she wondered, or for himself?

Asenath was wakened in the night by a bright light in her face and her mother's angry voice.

"Natha, I told you that woman was trouble. I caught her in the servants' quarters of the men. She must never come to this house again."

Asenath found her servant woman huddled in a corner. She reached to lift her to her feet, but Nophtet pulled away.

"They wanted me," she said fiercely. "They are servants of the sun priest, not the vizier.

"My parents do not wish for their men servants to share quarters with the women servants," Asenath explained patiently.

Nophtet looked at her friend imploringly. "I need to be loved," she said.

Helplessly, Asenath led her away to her own room for the night. There Nophtet lay upon a pallet on the floor and cried herself to sleep.

At breakfast the next morning a servant entered and bowed low. "The vizier sends a message that he wants his wife and sons to return home immediately. His father is coming."

CHAPTER 12

"Her children arise up and call her blessed;
her husband also, and he praiseth her."
Proverbs 31:28

Asenath had never seen Joseph in such agitation. He was waiting for her at the quay as the boat came to the shore, pacing and wringing his hands. He clasped her hands as soon as she stepped ashore. His aqua eyes were bright with a mixture of joy and apprehension.

"My father has come!" were his first words.

She smiled and nodded. "I'm happy for you," she said.

"He sent Judah ahead to me for directions to Goshen.[23] I sent Niki with him to show him the best land. How quickly can you be ready to go to Goshen?"

He wants me with him when he meets his father, she thought to herself. She felt the boys press against her as they listened to their father's exciting news. It's the boys that he wants with him, she amended the thought.

"We can leave now," she told him.

Joseph smiled gratefully. "Our tents and preparations are ready and in a wagon. We'll leave now in a chariot, and our things will follow. Come." He pulled her after him and the family climbed into a chariot which immediately hurried away to the east and the north.

Joseph didn't speak much as the chariot made a fast journey away from the city toward Goshen. He pulled the thick wig from his head and smoothed the golden hair. Manasseh and Ephraim chattered with enthusiasm about their grandfather. Asenath sat on the cushioned seat prepared for her and watched

---

[23] Genesis 46:28

the horizon ahead. Jehovah had truly brought Joseph's father to him. Excitement made a tight knot of her stomach. Joseph's brothers had been so different than anyone she knew. Curiosity gripped her, too, to meet a whole family who trusted in Joseph's God.

Before they reached the encampment of Joseph's family a band of little boys peered at them from behind palm trees. Suddenly they scurried away toward the camp. Manasseh and Ephraim pointed and shouted, "Look, boys!"

"Are they our cousins, Papa?" Manasseh asked.

Joseph was suddenly choked with emotion, but nodded assent. Asenath answered for him. "Yes, they are your cousins."

The boys whooped and strained to see them again, but they had disappeared.

Joseph had brought with them in the wagon the tent in which he had slept when working on the grain bins of Avis. It was a brass frame, tall enough for a man to stand erect, over which were draped heavy linen curtains, forming an enclosed structure. Asenath saw before them on the horizon a city of tents, but they were quite different than those she knew. These tents were low and sprawling, and made of brightly colored strips of animal skins sewed tightly together.

Asenath saw the bearded men dressed in long, flowing robes and colorful coats. From the distance she couldn't recognize any of them, but she knew that they were Joseph's brothers. She saw several women, some tending fires over which they cooked in pots suspended from tripods made of sticks. They wore long, brightly colored dresses. One woman rocked an animal skin back and forth on a stick suspended from a wooden tripod.

Children ran everywhere, and sheep, goats, and donkeys ran with them. Manasseh and Ephraim exclaimed excitedly about every new thing they observed.

The chariot came to a halt just inside the camp. Joseph stepped down and helped Asenath to the ground. Manasseh and

Ephraim jumped out, but stayed close to their parents. The cluster of men that had watched them approach drew near, and Asenath recognized the men who had been at her house. She saw Simeon among them, and he bowed his head toward her and smiled when she caught his eye.

The women and children stayed behind the men, but they crowded close to see and hear.

Then Asenath saw the old man in the center. His hair was white, and he limped as he walked toward the son he had so long thought was dead.[24] Joseph ran to him and embraced him weeping loudly. Father and son stood thus reunited for a long while.

When at last Joseph and his father, Jacob, unclasped, Joseph and his family were led to sit on mats in the shade of a tent which was spread above them like a canopy. Women came shyly and washed the feet of Joseph's family. Asenath suddenly wished that she had cared through the years to learn the Hebrew tongue from her husband, for she yearned to thank them, to be able to speak with these women. Manasseh and Ephraim, who knew much of their father's speech, began halting conversations with some little boys, and soon the children were talking and laughing gaily.

Joseph sat close to his father, and the two were engaged in conversation. Joseph called Manasseh and Ephraim to him, and presented them to his father, who embraced and kissed each. The boys sat at their grandfather's feet and listened to the old man and their father talking, forgetting their cousins for the moment. Joseph introduced Asenath, and she bowed before her father in law and smiled, but she couldn't understand his comment to her nor could she answer. She knew that Joseph explained, for Jacob merely nodded and smiled at her again.

Suddenly Nikansut was at her side, and he began to

---

[24] Genesis 32:31-32

translate for her. She smiled gratefully and listened carefully to the interpreted conversation as bowls of food were passed around. She was not at all hungry with her stomach knotted tightly, but she ate slowly, knowing that in courtesy she must.

"Now let me die, since I've seen your face, and I know that you're still alive," Jacob told Joseph.[25]

"The Lord God has been gracious and has brought you here to me," Joseph said to his father. "Many years were taken from us, but I trust that God will give us many years, yet."

"Tell me," Jacob said, "How is it that you are such a great man in Egypt?"

"The Lord God gave me the interpretation to Pharaoh's dreams when He told him that there would be seven years of plenty and then seven years of famine. Because the Lord gave me the interpretation, Pharaoh made me his vizier, second in command in the kingdom, and in charge of the gathering and dispersion of food."

Jacob nodded slowly. "And how did you come to be in Egypt?" he asked.

Asenath felt a wave of tension in the men seated about their father. They glanced nervously at Joseph, but he gave them a wry smile and winked.

"A band of Ishmaelites took me from Canaan to Egypt and sold me there as a slave."

Jacob nodded slowly without speaking. The answer seemed enough, for he asked no more about it.

"I see you dress as one of Egypt, as does your wife and your children," Jacob said.

"My wife is the daughter of Potiphera, priest of On. She is a worshipper of the gods of Egypt, as may be expected." Asenath felt her cheeks burning, and she strangely wished that she could then and there renounce the gods of Egypt and declare

---

[25] Genesis 46:30

faith in Jehovah alone.

Joseph smiled at Manasseh and Ephraim. "My sons trust and love the Lord God." He turned to his father. "We dress as do the Egyptians. I shave my face and wear a black wig of wool. We live in an Egyptian house and eat as Egyptians. In fact, our diet is such as the priests of Egypt follow. But we do nothing that pertains to the gods of Egypt." Joseph paused and looked sadly at Asenath. His words were hushed and heavy. "My wife venerates Egypt's gods, and therefore prays to them." He suddenly smiled at her. "But she submits to my wishes in our home, and does not interfere in my training of the boys to follow the Lord."

As Joseph talked with his father, Asenath's mind kept replaying his words of gentle praise, and she wished that he could be truly proud of her, as he was of his sons. He loved his sons. She wished that he could truly love her, too.

Simeon brought two women near to Asenath and introduced them as his two wives, Kael, and Lothri. They smiled shyly at her and she at them. She would learn the Hebrew tongue from Manasseh. She would study every day until she could speak with these women, wives to her husband's brothers.

"I will speak with Pharaoh and tell them that my father and brothers have come to me from the land of Canaan." Joseph was saying. "I'll tell him that you are shepherds and have brought your herds and flocks. I'm sure that Pharaoh will call you and want to speak with you. When he does, tell him that your trade has been to feed cattle and sheep. Then he won't make you move near the cities, but will let you live here, in the land of Goshen, for the Egyptians despise shepherds and won't live near them. Here is the best grazing for your animals."

Joseph and his family talked until the fires burned low and the embers glowed against the starry night. Asenath directed servants to carry her slumbering children to their tent and she joined them on the thick mats laid on the tent floor. She was very tired, but confusion nudged sleep from her as she considered

Joseph's God. He had shown Himself in power repeatedly, and now He once again showed His might. And Egypt's gods were silent.

The close air of the tent heated with the morning sun woke Asenath and she stepped outside to find the relief area. Then she wandered quietly between the bright tents of the Hebrews. A thought of Isis flitted across her mind, but she knew that if a chapel to Isis had been near she would not have gone to her to pray. She shaded her eyes against the rising sun and looked out on the great flock of sheep that dotted the plain before her.

"God of Joseph," she prayed, "You reunited my husband with the father he has so longed to see." She paused. "And still you scorch our land with famine. Yet, there is not one in Egypt or the lands near to us that must starve, for You have preserved food for them." She paused again, shutting her eyes hard in the quickly brightening light. "I am tempted to trust You, God of Joseph. But you know the fear in my heart of abandoning the gods of my people, my father's gods. Help me."

Women began to stir up the fires to bake the breakfast bread, and children emerged from tent doors rubbing the sleep from their eyes. Asenath joined her family to sit beneath the canopy. She listened to them speaking and felt awkward. Simeon's wives served her with blushing smiles. Joseph chose five of his brothers to accompany him to the palace at Memphis.[26]

Joseph embraced his father long. When he finally released the old man he turned quickly and climbed into his chariot. Joseph's brothers climbed into the wagon, and they turned southwest toward the city of Pharaoh. Manasseh and Ephraim shouted farewells to their cousins, who ran along beside them for awhile. Asenath watched the group of colorfully robed

---

[26] Genesis 47:2

men and women fade into the distance as they waved their arms in farewell.

****

Asenath paced, twisting her hands together. She wished that she could have gone, too, to see Apepi with Joseph's brothers, but she and the boys waited at home. Nophtet stood watching her pace.

"Go to your little chapel and pray to the gods," Nophtet suggested.

Asenath stopped pacing. "I have been praying since Joseph left."

"Do you pray to the God of the vizier?"

Asenath looked at her friend. "I have seen His power."

"But what of Egypt's gods?"

Asenath faltered. "I pray to Joseph's God when it concerns Joseph."

Joseph and his brothers celebrated when they returned from the Pharaoh's palace. Apepi had given Joseph's family the land of Rameses, the best of the land of Goshen. He had also offered the brothers of Joseph employment as herdsmen for his cattle in Goshen.[27]

With his family so close it was difficult for Joseph to stay in Memphis, but the world still beat a path to Egypt's door for grain, and Joseph must fulfill his duties. Asenath sat for hours every day as Manasseh patiently taught her the Hebrew tongue. Nikansut, who had picked the language up quickly from Joseph, also tutored her.

Joseph visited Goshen often and fell onto the bed each night greatly exhausted. His brothers often found their way to Joseph's home, and their table was frequently crowded with

---

[27] Genesis 47:6,11

guests at meals. Asenath longed for time to speak with Joseph of her growing trust in the Lord God, but opportunity did not come.

At last Jacob made the journey from the land of Goshen to the city of Pharaoh, and Joseph made a feast at his house. The Priest of On and his family were invited to join Joseph's father and brother's. The wives of his brothers came also, timidly hiding beneath veils and clinging closely together.

Asenath tried her awkward Hebrew with the women, and they smiled and chattered.

"Please, speak slowly," Asenath stuttered, and they tried to comply. Manasseh came to his mother's aid and served as interpreter when she could not grasp the strange words.

Asenath seated them in a cluster apart from the men, who were engaged in conversation. Servants came and washed the feet of the women. Nophtet carried a small bowl and towel for hand washing, and Asenath knew that she wanted a closer look at the women from Canaan.

Kael, the elder of Simeon's two wives, reached a calloused hand to grasp Asenath's delicate one. Her graying hair framed a kind face, and the corners of her eyes wrinkled in a smile. "My husband has told us of your kindness to him as he lay in the prison. Thank you. We feared for his life for we didn't know that the dreaded master of Egypt was his own brother. We praise God for his safe return to us."

"He spoke often of you and your children while in prison," Asenath told her, nodding toward Lothri as well. Lothri's dark eyes smiled, lighting her pretty face. She was darker than Kael, and Asenath decided that she was the Canaanite wife and mother of Shaul.

Zedek announced the arrival of Potiphera, and Asenath went to greet her family. They entered and bowed respectfully before the vizier, then sat upon the dais, apart from the Hebrews. Asenath saw the helpless look on her mother's face and the rigid set of her father's shoulders. But she smiled and chatted and tried to ease their tension. Nikansut joined them upon the dais as the servants came to wash their feet.

Servant women sat in a corner of the room and strummed soft chords from small harps. Large palm fronds were slowly waved above and behind the guests to circulate the warm air.

When the meal was served Asenath found herself flitting from the dais to the main floor to speak with both families. She had no chance to sit and eat at leisure, but visited a moment here before hurrying away there, so that none would feel neglected.

Joseph saw her frantic attempts and came to her, leading her to sit at his side by his father. She was grateful, but she kept casting watchful glances toward her family.

When the meal had been cleared away, Jacob turned his attention to the Priest of On. He raised his voice to traverse the distance between them.

"My son says that you are the priest of the Sun God."

Potiphera nodded his head once toward the old man.

"How is it that you see the wondrous works of the Lord God and still pray to gods of stone?"

Potiphera stared hard at Jacob as if he had not heard the question, but Jacob waited.

"Is a famine a wondrous work for a god to do?" Potiphera asked at last. "The gods of Egypt have never starved our people."

Jacob nodded his gray beard. "Yet it is a wondrous thing that none must starve in the famine, for the Lord God has given Egypt much grain."

Potiphera's stone facade did not falter. "I pray to gods that I can see and touch."

"The Lord God is infinite and cannot be seen by human eyes. Yet, I know Him as surely as I know Joseph," Jacob said, clapping Joseph on the back.

Potiphera's eyes glazed, and he stared, unspeaking. What was this hope Asenath cherished in her heart? She knew she sat watching the battle and hoping that her father would see the truth of Joseph's God, would trust in Jehovah. Was this she wished for him more than she herself could do? She closed her eyes on the scene and felt hot tears burn behind her eyelids.

When she opened her eyes she saw her mother's face, and an imploring glance met hers. My mother, too, wants my father to put his trust in Joseph's God, Asenath realized. She slipped from her place by Joseph and mounted the dais. Taking her mother's hand, she led her out of the crowded room to the rooftop garden.

"They are very different," Nofret said.

"They dress differently," Asenath said, "and they trust Joseph's God, but I think they aren't so different than you and I."

They watched the setting sun set the city of Memphis aglow. The eastern clouds blushed pink on the horizon.

Nofret spoke. "I believe that the vizier's God is the true God."

Asenath found herself smiling as she took her mother's hand. "Do you believe, Mama? Does Papa know this?"

Nofret turned sad eyes to her daughter. "How can I tell him? He is the priest of Ra. It would crush him to know his wife was not faithful to Egypt's gods."

"All of Papa's family now trust in the Lord God Jehovah," Asenath said. "Niki, and Ihat, and the boys have told Manasseh that they trust in the Lord, and now you."

"And you?" Nofret said.

Asenath watched the eastern clouds purple and fade to grey. "Yes, Mama, I also believe in the Lord God. I haven't even told Joseph, yet." She looked at Nofret. "Just now is the first time that I've admitted it, even to myself."

"Do you believe God answers prayer?" Nofret asked.

"I know He does," said Asenath.

"Then we must pray to God that your father will come to trust in Him, too."

The men departed to the palace to present Joseph's father to Apepi. Potiphera walked with them, and from the rooftop

Asenath saw his shoulders stooped in dejection.

"Let's go see to my guests, Mama, " she said, and they descended the stairs.

The women were washing their hands when Asenath and Nofret entered the room. They sat beside them and washed their hands as well. Nophtet stood after the other servants had left to hear what would be said. Asenath saw her, but did not send her away.

"This is my mother, Nofret," Asenath said. Then she introduced her sisters in law, stumbling over their strange sounding names. They nodded and smiled at Nofret and she at them. The conversation was slow and awkward until Asenath's two sons entered the room. Ephraim climbed on his grandmother's lap and Manasseh leaned against his mother's chair, both observing their unusual looking aunts.

"Do all of you believe in the Lord God, Jehovah?" Manasseh asked suddenly.

The women concurred and nodded assent. Nofret frowned at Asenath. "What did he ask them?" she said.

"I asked if they believe in the true and living God," Manasseh told his grandmother.

Nofret pulled him to her side and whispered in the child's ear, "Ask it of me, Manasseh."

"You?" he asked, his eyes wide in surprise.

"Yes, Manasseh, I believe in Jehovah, too."

The child hugged her excitedly, but suddenly ceased. "Does it anger Pippa that you trust my God?"

Nofret began to weep against the boy's hair. "I haven't told your Pippa."

Manasseh stroked his grandmother's black wig and soothed, "Don't worry. Papa and I have been praying for Pippa."

"Me, too," chimed in Ephraim as he patted Nofret's cheek.

The wives of Joseph's brothers silently watched the scene, unable to understand the dialogue. Asenath smiled at them and nodded. They smiled and returned nods.

Nophtet, standing near, cleared her throat, and Asenath looked at her. Her eyes were wide with dismay. Asenath dismissed her and she left the room in haste.

It seemed forever before Joseph and his brothers returned from the palace of Apepi. They sat on couches and cushions excitedly talking and the women sat beside them, or on rugs at their feet to hear. Joseph reached a hand to Asenath and she sat at his side.

"Apepi received my father as a very great man," he told her. "All Egypt reveres Pharaoh as a god, the Horus on earth, but Apepi accepted a blessing from my father."[28]

Asenath watched her father sit quietly in a corner of the room with Nofret at his side. He did not speak, but the expression he wore troubled Asenath. At last he stood and bowed toward Joseph.

"Thank you, Zaphnath, for honoring us with this meeting." He nodded toward Joseph's father and brothers. "We will depart."

"It's late." Joseph said. "You are welcome to rest for the night here."

Potiphera glanced at the great crowd in the room and smiled wryly. "My friend, Potiphar, will be glad to keep us for the night." He bowed low once more. Then, taking his wife's arm, he led her out of the house.

****

Ihat came to visit with a train of servants and begged Asenath to take her to Goshen to see the camp of the Hebrews there. Asenath had been to the Hebrew camp only once, that first day with Joseph. Manasseh and Ephraim heard Ihat's pleas

---

[28] Genesis 47:10

and joined her in imploring their mother for a visit to the Hebrew camp.

Joseph could not accompany them, but he eagerly gave them leave to go. They left early in the morning with wagons and servants, and arrived in the late afternoon. Asenath had practiced much and felt much more comfortable with her Hebrew speech.

Joseph's family was delighted that she had come, and insisted that she leave her tent in the wagon and use their tents. They were shown to several sprawling tents, which were divided into several sleeping compartments, each piled with soft furs and skins for sleeping.

"Welcome, Asenath," Jacob greeted her when she emerged from a tent. She bowed low before her father in law, and he motioned for her to sit at his side.

The old man considered the young woman. He had little knowledge of the ways of Egypt, but he excused her heavy makeup and strange dress. He was a man who had met the Lord face to face, and a great concern weighted his heart that Joseph was wed to a pagan woman.

"My son loves and trusts the Lord Jehovah with all of his heart," he said to her.

"Yes," she responded, looking into eyes as blue green as Joseph's own. "His God is his very life."

"And you," said Jacob, "do you believe in Jehovah God's power?"

She continued to look into his gaze. "I believe in the Lord God, Jehovah."

Jacob squinted. "My son told me that you revere the gods of Egypt."

"Joseph has been so very busy. I haven't told him, yet, that I believe in his God." Seeing the look of disbelief in the man's eyes she hurried on. "It's by your own coming to Egypt that the Lord God, Jehovah has shown Himself to me. I have for some time believed that He could answer prayer. It was only when he brought you to Joseph that I turned from Egypt's gods to Jehovah in faith." Asenath wondered at the declaration she had made to her father in law, for she had not put it into words thus before.

"But you have not told Joseph?"

"No."

"He is very busy serving Egypt. But he's not too busy to hear what you have to tell him. Don't you realize how much he waits to hear those words from you? Do you know how much he has prayed for you to believe in Jehovah?"

Asenath lowered her eyes. "Yes, I know."

"Tomorrow you must return to him. You must tell him."

When Asenath found her sister and sons, Ihat sat listening intently as Manasseh interpreted the conversation around her. She smiled at Asenath, pulling her to sit at her side.

"Do you see that man?" she asked, nodding toward a young man sitting at the edge of the camp watching the grazing sheep.

"Yes."

"He is Simeon's son, Shaul," Ihat told her. "S h a u l, what a strange and beautiful name."

Asenath looked at Ihat with a question.

"He saw me as he passed to his sheep, and stopped to talk with me. He knew no Egyptian and I very little Hebrew, but his smile was so gorgeous! Somehow, we communicated without words."

"Ihat!" Asenath reproved. "Papa has found you a husband. You will soon be wed."

Ihat turned her large, beautiful eyes to her sister. "Shaul is Jacob's grandson. He is a believer in Jehovah. I would rather spend my life as the wife of a believer of Jehovah, even in a tent such as this," she raised her arm to span the camp, "than as the wife of a priest of On," she declared.

Asenath was silent for a moment. "Ihat," she said softly, "I, too, believe in Jehovah."

Ihat's face lit in joy. "The vizier must be so happy!"

"I haven't told him, yet."

"Why?"

"Since I've placed my faith in Jehovah alone I haven't had a chance. Jacob told me that I must return tomorrow, and tell him." "Tomorrow?" said Ihat, alarmed. "I thought that we could spend several days here."

"We must go tomorrow."

Asenath lay on the soft bed that night listening to the lowing of the cattle and the rustling of movement in the field beyond the camp. Asenath knew her sister dreamed of a young man who stood guard over beast and family in the darkness tonight. Such unusual things had come into their lives. She was an Egyptian woman. She lay upon Egyptian soil beneath the Egyptian sky, but her heart now throbbed for the Lord God, the Creator of heaven and earth, the God of these strange people. The God of Joseph. Asenath was suddenly seized with the great desire to see Joseph, to tell him of her faith in his God. As sleep drew her into its numbing arms she remembered and pulled away to sit up, wide awake. Would Joseph love her, now that she trusted his God? A thrill coursed through her, and she lay again, but couldn't sleep.

Asenath heard a soft titter outside the tent. It came again, and she sat up suddenly. She knew that voice, even without utterance of words. She threw a robe of fur about her and went out into the night. Carefully picking her way around tent stakes and ropes in the darkness, she approached the sound.

She heard a sharp gasp as someone rose up from the ground at her side. She clutched clothing in the darkness, and someone scurried away between the tents. But in her grasp she held her friend and servant, Nophtet.

Asenath's eyes were growing accustomed to the darkness, and she could see the defiance in Nophtet's eyes. Her clothing was hanging away from her body, and she pulled it about her as she faced Asenath.

"Why?" was all that Asenath found to say.

"I am a woman!" Nophtet whispered fiercely. "I need to be loved."

"That isn't love, Nophtet," Asenath said dismally. Her tone hardened. "I demand that you stay away from the men of this camp."

"He came to me," Nophtet pouted.

"I wish to keep you as my servant," Asenath said, avoiding the word "companion." "But I can't tolerate this behavior."

"It's as I've always behaved," Nophtet said.

"Please," Asenath appealed. "Such behavior lost you your rank and position and almost your life."

"I have no husband to wrong, now,"

"Please," Asenath entreated again. "Don't do this."

"Then it would have been better to die," Nophtet said bitterly.

"You need love, but this is not love."

"Then where shall one such as I find love?"

Asenath bit her lip. "Trust is Jehovah God, the Creator of heaven and earth. He loves you. He will fill the void and meet your need."

"So, it's true. You, too, believe in the vizier's God."

"Yes," Asenath told her, "and if you will put your trust in Him, you'll know real love."

Nophtet's shoulders sagged. "I have never really put my trust in anything, not even the gods of Egypt. How does one trust in the vizier's invisible God?"

Indeed, thought Asenath, how could it be explained? She only knew that she had come to trust Jehovah. How could she make Nophtet understand?

"I can't explain," she said, "I only know that I trust Him, and He answers my prayers."

"Do you suggest that I should pray to Him?" Nophtet asked in derision.

"Yes."

Nophtet looked at her curiously, then bowed low and retreated to her tent.

After a breakfast of flat bread baked on hot stones and warm milk fresh from the goats, Asenath said goodbye to her sisters in law and their families. She bowed before her father in law and he blessed her as she readied to depart.

"Go with God, and may He bless you for the faith that you have placed in Him."

She found Ihat at the edge of the camp near the sheep talking shyly to a sleepy shepherd. As they walked away toward their wagon she teased gently, "Shaul's eyes are brown, not blue green as his father's."

"Yes, and I think they're beautiful eyes."

"I thought you wanted a man with eyes like the viziers'."

"How silly to care what color a man's eyes are," Ihat said, smiling.

As they travelled the long journey back to Memphis, Ihat mourned her father's choice for her.

"Do you think Papa could change his mind and give me in marriage to Shaul, instead?" she asked.

Asenath only shook her head sadly. Such a thing was definitely not a possibility.

"Niki told me that the Lord once told the vizier's grandfather, Abraham, that nothing is impossible with the Lord,"[29] Ihat said. "I will pray to Jehovah. He can change our father's mind."

"It is our father's heart that needs to change," Asenath told her.

"He can change that, too," said Ihat.

When the weary party entered the gate to the stables of Joseph, Zedek met Asenath.

---

[29] Genesis 18:14

"The master has gone to Giza," he told her. "Potiphera has climbed aloft the Great Pyramid Temple."

Asenath was puzzled. Why would Joseph go to the Temple of the Mysteries?

Zedek perceived her confusion. "Your father is at the top of the pyramid."

Asenath frowned. Still she didn't understand. She knew little of the rituals of the Mysteries, but she wasn't surprised to learn that her father was appealing to Egypt's gods.

"It is feared that he plans to take his life," Zedek said.

CHAPTER 13

"Favor is deceitful, and beauty is vain: but a woman that feareth the Lord, she shall be praised." Proverbs 31:30

Nikansut held his anguishing mother at the base of the Great Pyramid Temple. Ipi and Wehemki started climbing the treacherous slick face of the pyramid, but Nikansut called them back. The Initiates of the Mysteries were gathered at the corner of the structure wearing long, hooded robes.

Asenath and Ihat embraced their mother and brothers and then turned their eyes upward to the pinnacle of the pyramid. There, far above the sandy plain, seated astride the capstone, was Egypt's primary priest, the high priest of On. The evening sun glinted off the polished face of the pyramid as Egypt's vizier, moving slowly and cautiously along the slippery surface, ascended toward Potiphera.

"Papa!" Ihat cried.

"Joseph!" Asenath echoed. She watched him moving slowly, knowing well that one slip could send him plummeting to his death.

She kept her eyes on Joseph, but breathed a prayer. "Jehovah, God, protect Joseph as he climbs the height of this pyramid. Hold him to the surface, please don't let him fall."

"Let Joseph reach my father," Niki took up the prayer. "Let my father listen to the words of Joseph."

"Make him listen, O Lord God," Nofret prayed. "His heart and soul are sore grieved at the failure of Egypt's gods. Show him Who You are. Make him let go of his gods and trust in You."

The family of the sun god's priest continued in prayer to Jehovah as Joseph made his way closer. The Enlightened Ones of the Mysteries watched, soundlessly. They had come to the end of their powers and prayers. Their superior had lost all hope, and their hearts had ascended with him in despair. Potiphar separated from the cluster of men and approached Potiphera's family. He stood quietly, listening to their supplications to the God of Joseph and watching Joseph's ascent.

When they paused in their prayers, Potiphar spoke. "The gods will not answer," he said sadly. "We have invoked them in every way that we know. The blood of beasts and men has flowed in abundance, and we have sacrificed dearly. But the gods will not answer. We have been faithful, but this famine rages on, and the gods have done nothing." He looked at Nikansut, explaining. "He is not giving up. He is willing to make the ultimate sacrifice. If the offering of his own life will bring an answer from the gods, he is willing to do it. For you, for Egypt."

Nofret began to weep softly. Nikansut grasped the older man's arm. "There is nothing that can end the famine. It is the Lord God Jehovah Who foretold and delivered the famine. I have put my trust in Him. That is the answer. For my father. For you. For everyone."

Everyone held his breath as Joseph reached the summit and placed his feet against the capstone. All were hushed, but no words carried to them from the great height. The silence pressed upon those waiting below.

The sun slipped below the horizon with a blaze of brilliance, and the sky slowly dimmed to purple-black. And still the family clutched on the sand prayed.

The evening star winked down upon the anxious gathering and was soon joined by a myriad of twinkling points. But they leant no light to the eager eyes that were lifted into the inky blackness. At last the moon rose and began her slow arc of the night sky. By the faint light of the moon, the watchers saw movement along the sheer side of the pyramid.

A murmur coursed through the vigil, but silence resumed as they strained eyes to watch the descent.

"Bring them both down to safety, Lord," Asenath prayed. Hours had slipped away in the tension when at last two figures loomed just above them on the sloping surface of the pyramid. Everyone gathered below them in case of a slip on the final descent.

Joseph placed his foot down on the foundation stone first and reached to aid Potiphera in the last step to safety. The family climbed up onto the foundation and encircled the two men with embraces.

Asenath could not see her father's face well in the low light, but she squeezed him tightly, and he responded with a squeeze. She slipped her hand into Joseph's, and he swept her into his arms, burying his face against her neck. His body trembled against her.

"I prayed to Jehovah for you," she whispered. "We all prayed."

"Praise the Lord," he answered, still trembling. "I've never been so scared in my life."

"My father?"

"Let him tell you," Joseph said. He helped her down to the ground, and the family made their way down from the foundation. The priests and other onlookers solemnly gathered around their high priest at the foot of the Great Pyramid.

Nofret and Ihat leaned against Potiphera as he faced his family and companions.

"I have ever been a faithful priest to the gods of Egypt," the Priest of On began. "My whole life has been dedicated to their service." His eyes were wet and tears coursed along his face. He looked at his son, Nikansut. "I devotedly followed the Mysteries of Egypt. Nothing that was asked of me was denied. I obeyed without question." Nikansut nodded, reaching to grasp his father's hand, for he understood the turmoil in his father's heart. The Initiates crowded closer, for they, too, comprehended this.

"When the famine came to Egypt," Potiphera continued,

"my gods turned a deaf ear to my pleas. I was faithful to them, but they deserted me." He turned his eyes toward Joseph, and a smile played about his mouth. "Manasseh told me that my gods were idols of stone, unable to hear and answer my prayers. And he was right. But I continued to pray to them, to no avail."

"When Niki turned from my gods, my heart broke, but I couldn't blame him. Egypt's gods had failed him. Zaphnath's God saved him." Potiphera let his eyes scan the faces before him. "One by one my family turned from my gods to Zaphnath's God." His gaze rested on Nofret, leaning against him. "Even my wife," he said softly. She looked into his eyes uncertainly, but he smiled.

"You did not need words to tell me," he told her, "I knew. And then Zaphnath's father came to Egypt." He looked at his son in law again. "Jacob asked me, 'How is it that you see the wondrous works of the Lord God and still pray to gods of stone?' My heart cried out the same question, but my stubborn pride held me firm in my devotion to Egypt's gods. Until my heart could wait no more, and I resolved to offer the supreme sacrifice to my gods."

He surveyed his family once more. "That is why I climbed the Temple Pyramid. My plan was to cast myself before my gods. They must respect such a sacrifice and intervene for Egypt. But as I sat aloft, I knew that they would not, they could not, for they were only idols of stone, and cared not for Egypt. When Zaphnath came to me there, I had already denounced Egypt's deities. Zaphnath taught me of Jehovah, and I pledged my faith to Him." He looked at the hooded priests gathered near. "The priest of the sun god has trusted in Jehovah, God of heaven and earth."

When Potiphera ceased his recitation, the family embraced him again, weeping with him. Potiphera turned away from the burial grounds of Giza and returned to On.

When the family had gone toward the house of Potiphera, Asenath took Joseph's hand and led him along the quay.

"All of my father's family now trusts in the Lord God," she said.

Joseph nodded. "Praise God," he said softly.

"All of us, Joseph."

Joseph reached his hands and cupped her face, peering into her eyes in the light of the moon. "You, Asenath?" he whispered.

She put her hands against his and nodded. "Yes, I have put my trust in the Lord, Jehovah."

"What of Egypt's gods?" Joseph asked.

"I know that they have no power. They are, as you have said, only gods of stone."

Joseph folded her in his arms. His body trembled against hers. He was weeping! Asenath held him tightly, waiting for the emotion to pass.

"I have prayed so long for you to trust in the Lord God," he said with difficulty.

"I know." Asenath said. She pulled the chain from which hung the ankh up over her head and held the amulet in her hand. "I no longer need this," she said.

Joseph took the amulet from her hand. "Are you sure?" he asked. She nodded. He pitched the amulet and chain far out over the dark waters. They arched up silently and then fell with only a soft splash. Joseph and Asenath stood watching the waters of the Nile River shimmer silver in the moonlight.

"Your father told me that he will soon speak with Apepi, for he cannot remain a priest of the sun god."

"What will he do?"

"He doesn't know. But he will move away from the city of On with its temple to the sun god."

"What will Pharaoh think of this?"

"We can only pray and wait to see."

As they stood together talking, Asenath's heart was crying out, "I believe in your God. Can you now love me?" But she couldn't form it into spoken words.

****

Potiphera entered the throne room of Pharaoh Apepi with great pomp, followed by family, servants, and fellow priests. The king stood atop the steps which led to his throne and watched them assemble before him. The twinkle was absent from his green eyes, and Asenath knew she had never seen his expression so grim.

News had preceded the priest of On to the king. But he waited to hear it from the man himself. Potiphera and his assembly bowed before the king, and then Potiphera mounted the steps to stand before Apepi. Always he had revered the Pharaoh as the Horus on earth, but now he stood before a mortal man.

"Do you have a message for me, priest of Ra?" Apepi asked.

"I do, my king," Potiphera answered, nodding his head low. "You know that I have been a faithful priest to Egypt's gods, even when this famine came and I could get no answer from them. I have followed the Mysteries of Egypt with great devotion. I have answered every summons without question." He lowered his voice. "I have shed men's blood in submission to the directives of the Mysteries. But when famine came, and I pled with the gods, offering all that I could, there was no response from them. They continued to allow the God of Zaphnathpaaneah to receive recognition for bringing the famine upon us. They would not end the famine and give Egypt bread."

Potiphera stepped up another step to put him at eye level with the king. "And now I know why," he said. "I now understand that the gods of Egypt are idols of stone, unable to hear and answer prayers. Only the Lord God, Jehovah, is God. Only He can hear and answer prayers. He has brought this famine upon us, and we must wait its fulfillment, and thank Him that there is bread in Egypt."

Silence crowded tightly about the room, suffocating

Asenath as her heart raced. She knew that such a claim could bring the guard of Pharaoh down upon her father and consign him to prison. His station as high priest could not save him, for he had denounced the gods of Egypt.

Apepi's eyes sought Joseph in the crowd, and he called him to his side. "When the God of Zaphnathpaaneah gave me dreams that none else could interpret, I gave Him due honor. I myself cannot disclaim Egypt's gods, for I am the Horus on earth, representative of those gods. But, I cannot argue that the God of Zaphnathpaaneah has done something which cannot be explained." Pharaoh looked at the former sun priest. "If the highest priest of Egypt trusts in the God of Zaphnathpaaneah, then I, as divine agent, must declare Him a God indeed." His eyes swept the assembly before him. "All who wish to worship the God of Zaphnathpaaneah will do so with my blessing." He looked again at his priest. "Will you transfer, then, to a new temple, dedicated to the veneration of Jehovah?"

"No, my king, for Jehovah doesn't need a building made with hands. He will hear the prayers of His faithful anywhere, anytime."

Apepi consulted Joseph. "Is this so? Do you wish no temple to Jehovah?"

"It is so."

And so it was. Potiphera was released from the priesthood of Egypt with the blessing of the Pharaoh. He moved his family and household from the city of the sun to live near his son in law. Apepi, in a gesture of great graciousness, allowed Potiphera to retain his farm lands. After the move, the first venture of the former priest of On was to journey to Goshen to speak with Jacob, Joseph's father. He sought knowledge of Jehovah as fervently as ever he had worshipped the gods of Egypt.

****

Asenath sat beside an open window deftly weaving an ornate mat from river grasses. The sun warmed her, and a breeze caught her breath. She paused and stared over the city, pondering the changes that had come to her family. A muted cough brought her attention to Nophtet, who stood dutifully at her side.

"Nophtet?" she asked.

Nophtet bowed and then knelt before her. "Madame, I must admit my astonishment that your honorable father has turned from the gods of Egypt to the vizier's God." She lowered her eyes. "I know that I have done much evil. And I know that your God desires purity and goodness." She raised eyes brimming with tears to Asenath. "I have not purity nor goodness. But I desire to put my faith in your God." She collapsed in tears at Asenath's feet.

Asenath put her hand on her friend's head. "It doesn't matter what we are like when we come to Jehovah in faith. If we will trust in Him, He will forgive us for everything that we have done that displeases Him." Asenath spoke confidently to her friend the words that she had heard spoken by her husband and by her sons, and she hoped that she spoke them correctly.

Nophtet looked at her again. "Will Jehovah accept my prayers?"

"Yes," Asenath said, embracing her friend and then kneeling to pray with her.

The two women still knelt in prayer when a servant announced the arrival of Ihat. Nophtet squeezed Asenath's hands gratefully and left the room. Ihat entered with sunshine in her smile. She knelt on the floor as her habit was, and placing her arms in Asenath's lap, she smiled into her face.

"Papa has voided my betrothal to the young priest of Ra. He said it is his will that I marry a man who believes in Jehovah! So, will you pray with me that Shaul will be the one?"

Asenath laughed and hugged her sister. "I will, little sister."

"Are you and the vizier happy, now?" Ihat asked.

Asenath blushed. "Why do you ask? I've been content for many years."

"But now that you trust in his God, is he happy at last?"

"Yes," Asenath answered, but the question was unanswered in her heart.

That evening Joseph ascended the steps to the living quarters of his home wearily, as he had so many times. The nations of the world clamoured at Egypt's grain bins for sustenance, and none would be denied, but it took a toll on the man who must see to the dispensing. He pulled off his wig as usual and scratched his head. As he reached the top step he found his wife waiting. He reached to take her hand and lead her into the house, but she stopped.

"I want you to come with me to Isis," she told him. His eyes opened wide in question, but he followed her down the stairs to the tiny chapel hidden behind the animal pens.

"I will never again pray to idols of stone," Asenath told him. "Will you take this away?"

Joseph suddenly embraced her. "I was worried. I thought..." but his words trailed away.

She smiled at him. "I truly believe in the Lord God Jehovah, Creator of heaven and earth."

Joseph lifted the small chapel and idol and carried them to the pavement beside the pool. There he hefted them high above his head and sent them crashing to the ground, where they splintered apart. Joseph fetched a course grain bag and shovel. He lifted the fragments into the bag and carried it into a field, where he buried it beneath the sand of Egypt.

When he had shovelled the last to cover it, the sun was setting. He reached for Asenath and held her. "I'm so happy," he said. "The Lord God has answered my prayers for you."

****

A long train walked away from the city of On across the desert sands. Zedek dutifully carried a bellowing lamb to the altar of Joseph. There Joseph repaired the altar of rough stones. Then, facing the assembly, he told the stories once more of Adam and Eve and their sin against God. He told how the Lord shed the blood of a lamb to clothe them, signifying the blood of Messiah, which would one day be shed for the sin of mankind. Joseph then knelt and stroked the head of the lamb before quickly slitting its throat. As its life drained into a basin, Joseph explained that as the life is in the blood, so the shedding of blood brings forgiveness of sin. Potiphera and Nofret, new to the sacrifices made to Jehovah, gathered nearer to Joseph with their children. As the gathering knelt on the desert floor, Nophtet bowed with them, and Asenath at Joseph's side. When the coals were shaken from the brazier onto the wood beneath the sacrifice, Asenath did not draw away. She breathed in the sharp odder of the fire against the sacrifice, and she thanked the Lord God.

When the sacrifices to Jehovah had burned to ashes, Joseph and Asenath walked through the cooling sand away from the family who sat talking in the waning light.

"Joseph, I love you," Asenath said suddenly. "I've wanted you to love me for such a long time, but I wouldn't give up the gods of Egypt." Joseph stopped walking and his blue-green eyes were intense. She continued, the tears stinging her eyes, "I believe in your God, now. Can you love me?"

Joseph's voice broke as he spoke. "I've always loved you, ever since we met on our wedding day." He shook his head slightly. "Forgive me if I never made my love known to you."

"But you so often got so angry with me."

"Because I wanted so much for you to turn from your idols and trust in Jehovah. It was because I love you that I wanted that so badly."

Asenath looked down, away from those earnest eyes. "Someone has observed to me that you have not been happy."

Joseph lifted her chin and smiled. "You have made me happy. You've been faithful and obedient, even when it wasn't your way or your will. You gave me two sons," his voice trembled, "and you respected my wish that they not be taught in Egypt's religion." He paused. "You are my best friend." Asenath recalled the words of Apepi, on her wedding day, and warmed.

"If anything in my life made me unhappy," Joseph said, "it was that you didn't trust in the Lord God. But I've always loved you." Joseph folded Asenath into his arms and kissed away her tears. She knew he loved her. And she loved him.

At last, their two hearts were one.

Epilogue

The true story of Joseph and his family is told in the last fourteen chapters of Genesis in the Bible. When the seven years of famine came to an end, the family continued on in Goshen in the land of Egypt. Four generations later, when a pharaoh reigned who did not remember Joseph or the famine of his days, the family of Joseph, then called the children of Israel, were made to be slaves to the Egyptians. The book of Exodus in the Bible tells how God delivered the children of Israel out of Egypt and guided them on their way back to Canaan, the Promised Land.

Many years later, through the family of Judah, the Messiah came, as promised. His name was Jesus Christ. He lived a miraculous life and died a bloody death on the cross to pay the penalty for man's sin. After three days in the grave, Jesus Christ arose to life again, conquering death, and making the way to eternal life for every person.

"For God so loved the world that he gave his only begotten Son, that whosoever believeth in him should not perish, but have everlasting life." John 3:16.